The Dead Fathers Club

The Dead Fathers Club

MATT HAIG

VIKING

VIKING
Published by the Penguin Group
Penguin Group (USA) Inc., 375 Hudson Street, New York, New York 10014, U.S.A.
Penguin Group (Canada), 90 Eglinton Avenue East, Suite 700, Toronto, Ontario, Canada
M4P 2Y3 (a division of Pearson Penguin Canada Inc.)
Penguin Books Ltd, 80 Strand, London WC2R 0RL, England
Penguin Ireland, 25 St. Stephen's Green, Dublin 2, Ireland (a division of Penguin Books Ltd)
Penguin Books Australia Ltd, 250 Camberwell Road, Camberwell, Victoria 3124, Australia
(a division of Pearson Australia Group Pty Ltd)
Penguin Books India Pvt Ltd, 11 Community Centre, Panchsheel Park,
New Delhi – 110 017, India
Penguin Group (NZ), Cnr Airborne and Rosedale Roads, Albany, Auckland 1310, New
Zealand (a division of Pearson New Zealand Ltd)
Penguin Books (South Africa) (Pty) Ltd, 24 Sturdee Avenue, Rosebank,
Johannesburg 2196, South Africa

Penguin Books Ltd, Registered Offices:
80 Strand, London WC2R 0RL, England

First American edition
Published in 2007 by Viking Penguin,
a member of Penguin Group (USA) Inc.

1   3   5   7   9   10   8   6   4   2

Publisher's Note
This is a work of fiction. Names, characters, places, and incidents either are the product of the author's imagination or are used fictitiously, and any resemblance to actual persons, living or dead, business establishments, events, or locales is entirely coincidental.

ISBN 978-0-670-03833-6

Printed in the United States of America
Set in Goudy
Designed by Spring Hoteling

The Dead Fathers Club

The First Time I Saw
Dad After He Died

I walked down the hall and pushed the door and went into the smoke and all the voices went quiet like I was the ghost.

Carla the Barmaid was wearing her hoop earrings and her tired eyes. She was pouring a pint and she smiled at me and she was going to say something but the beer spilt over the top.

Uncle Alan who is Dads brother was there wearing his suit that was tight with his neck pouring over like the beer over the glass. His big hands still had the black on them from mending cars at the Garage. They were over Mums hands and Mums head was low like it was sad and Uncle Alans head kept going down and he lifted Mums head up with his eyes. He kept talking to Mum and he looked at me for a second and he saw me but he didnt say anything. He just looked back at Mum and kept pouring his words that made her forget about Dad.

Nan was sitting on her own with her silver sticks on the seat and she was drinking red juice like blood in her glass.

Her eyes went in a squint and made her face more wrinkly

and she saw me. Her skeleton hand said Come here come here so I went and sat with her and she just stared at me and didnt say anything at first. She just looked round at everyone and went Sssss because of her pains like she had a puncture.

After a bit she said Ee now come on pet dinny you fret. It will be all right son.

Nan lives in Sunderland and she speaks Sunderlanguage. Mum used to live in Sunderland but she hates it and says it is a Ghost Town and she doesnt talk Sunderlanguage only a bit when she talks to Nan but most of the time she talks normal.

Nan said Youre not a little bairn now son. Youre the man of the place.

I am 11 so I am not a little bairn and I am not a man but I didnt say anything I just nodded my head a bit and Carla came and gave me a glass of Pepsi.

Carla said in her croaky frog voice Theres a glass of Pepsi duck.

She put it on the table and smiled at me with her thin lips and she itched the dryness on her arm and then smiled at Nan and she went back to the bar.

Nan kept on saying things and I just drank my Pepsi and looked round at the people. I think most of them were happy that the Pub was open and they were talking louder than at the funeral because funerals make voices quiet and beer makes voices loud so now they were speaking about normal.

The Regulars were there like Big Vic and Les who were at the bar and smoking Hamlet cigars and speaking to Carla.

Carla always talked to men since her Divorce and since she stopped falling over and getting the bruises. Mum used to tell Dad she thought Carla was an Old Tart but she liked her really. I dont know if Carla is older than Mum because she has twins in my Year at school but she looks older than Mum.

Les didnt look happy but Les never looks happy and that is why Dad always called him Les Miserable. And when I was looking at them Big Vic looked at me and normally when he looked at me he smiled or said something funny like Oi Philip its your round. But that day he looked away as soon as his eyes touched my eyes as if looking at my eyes could be dangerous or make him ill or as if my eyes had lasers in them that cut him in half.

I moved my eyes and watched Mum and Uncle Alan and I wanted Uncle Alans hands to stop holding Mums hands and they did stop when Renuka went and talked to Mum. Renuka is Mums best friend who goes to Step class with her on Mondays and Thursdays where they step on boxes for an hour to make their bums smaller. Renuka had been with Mum lots this week and she had made 700 cups of tea and Uncle Alan looked cross now because when Renuka talks no one can fit words in because she doesnt have any spaces.

I kept looking round the bar and Nan kept talking to me and that is when I saw him. That is when I saw Dads Ghost.

King of the CASTLE

You are meant to be frightened when you see a ghost but I was not frightened because it felt completely normal which is weird because I had never seen a ghost before. He was just standing there behind the smoke of Big Vics cigar and he was looking at me and not scared of my eyes like everyone else was.

Carla was next to him serving drinks but she didnt notice him and I looked round and no one noticed him apart from me. After she had served the drinks Carla walked through Dads Ghost to go and see herself in the mirror which says Castle and Falcon because that is the name of our Pub.

Dads Ghost was wearing the same clothes Dad was wearing the last time I saw him which was at breakfast on the day he died when I made him cross because I wanted the PlayStation. He was wearing his T shirt which said King of the Castle with the word CASTLE written in red capital letters like on the sign outside the Pub. But now all the colours were more faded because Dad was pale and see through like the ghosts at the

Haunted Mansion in Disney World and he had blood running down from his hair.

Nan asked me Whats the matter pet?

She turned to see where I was looking but she couldnt see anything and Dads Ghost was now telling me to follow him with his hand.

I said to Nan I need the toilet.

I went past the bar and down the hall and into the back office where Dads Ghost walked through the door.

I checked to see if anyone was looking and they werent so I opened the door because I couldnt walk through it and Dads Ghost was standing in the corner by the desk and the computer was on which was weird.

He nodded to the door and so I shut it and then he said Dont be scared.

I said Im not.

His voice sounded the same but different like he was standing far away but I could hear him more clearly than ever. That doesnt make sense but that is how he sounded.

And the second thing he said was Im sorry.

I said For what?

He said For everything.

And when he said it I thought he was talking about the past when he was alive but now I am not sure.

I went across the room and I went to touch him and my hand went right through and I couldnt feel anything except a bit warmer but I might have just been thinking that.

I dont think Dads Ghost liked me doing it but he didnt say anything but I didnt do it again.

I said Are you a ghost?

It was a stupid question but I didnt know what to say.

He said Yes.

I said Where have you been?

He said I am not here all the time. I go on and off.

And I said Like a light bulb?

And he smiled but in a sad way and he said Yes like a light bulb. It is hard to control where I go but I am getting better.

And I said Have you been to the Pub before?

He nodded his head and said You were asleep.

Then I asked him if he sees other ghosts and he said There are lots of ghosts in Newark and they take some getting used to because they are all from different ages.

And I said It must be weird seeing all the ghosts.

He said It is.

Then he was quiet for a second and then he said Philip.

So I said What?

But really I didnt want to know because I could tell from his voice that he was going to say something bad like when Grandad died.

He said I have to tell you something.

And then he stopped for a minute and looked at the door and I wondered why he was looking at the door but then Uncle Alan walked in and he never walks into the office and Uncle Alan looked at the computer and he said Your mum sent me to look for you.

And he was smiling and his big hands were holding his glass of whisky on his big stomach. And he went over and touched my shoulder and he said Are you all right Philip?

And I said Yes.

And he said Its been a tough day for all of us.

I said Yes.

I just wanted him to stop touching my shoulder.

I could see Dads Ghost looking at him and he was looking at him in a way I had never seen him look at anyone before especially not his brother and I knew he didnt like him being in the office. So I said Ill go out in a minute Im just looking for something.

And Uncle Alan sighed and made the air smell of whisky and he was going to say something but he wasnt my Dad and so he went out again and shut the door.

Then I looked at Dads Ghost who was flickering and screaming but with the volume down and then he came back and he said I might not have long.

Then he faded out for about five seconds and came back.

He tried to speak and all I could hear was It wasnt

And then he tried again and again.

It wasnt

It

It was

It wasnt

It wasnt an axe

He disappeared and I said Dad Dad Dad! Come back! Come back!

But he didnt.

Then I heard a voice say Oh Philip and it was my mums voice and I dont know how long she had been there and Uncle Alan was now behind her and touching her shoulder but she didnt feel the coldness down her back like I did.

The Bad News

Dad died because his car crashed into a bridge outside of Kelham which is a village near Newark. There was a picture of it on East Midlands Today and it showed the whole car hanging over the edge like it was going to fall into the River Trent. All the windows were smashed like spiders webs and the woman on the news was talking about the bridge having to be closed for two months as if the bridge was the important thing.

Before we saw the news there was a policeman who came to the back door and I knew the policeman because he had been into the Pub before talking to Dad. The policeman had a face like an empty plate and he opened and closed his mouth for a long time with nothing coming out but air.

I was watching from the top of the stairs and they couldnt see me and I couldnt hear them properly but I knew something was wrong from the way the policeman had his hat on his chest.

And then they went into the office and shut the door and I could hear nothing for ages and then I heard Mum. She was howling like a WOLF and the noise hurt my stomach and I closed my eyes to try and hear the policeman and all he was saying was Im sorry and he kept on saying it

Im sorry

Im sorry

Im sorry

and I knew that he hadnt done anything wrong because he was a policeman and policemen only say sorry if something very bad has happened. So I knew right then what the pain in my stomach was. And I saw the policeman leave and the hat was in his hand but not on his chest any more like the Bad News had been in there and set free. And I saw Mum and she saw me but didnt see me properly and she went to the corner of the hall by the radiator and sat down in a ball and cried and shook her head in her hands and said No no no no no and everywhere round us looked the same but bigger and I wanted to go and tell her it was OK but that would have been a lie and so I just sat there and did nothing.

The Terrors

Dads Ghost came back later on when everyone had left the Pub and I was in my bedroom.

Dads Ghost flickered on and at first he looked like he was in too much pain to speak but then he said Philip dont be scared of me.

I said Im not.

He said I have to tell you someth

He flickered out and then came back.

He said It wasnt an accident.

I said What?

He said It wasnt an accident son.

I said What do you mean?

He said Look out of the window.

I said What?

He said Look out of the window.

I got up out of the bed and I got inside the curtain and I

looked out at the car park and the street light showed it was empty except for the Ka car.

He said Can you see them?

I said Who?

He said There by the Bottle Banks.

I looked at the three Bottle Banks that the Council made Dad put at the back of the car park.

I looked on the left side and there was a shopping trolley with a plastic bag trapped in one of the wheels and it was flapping in the wind like it wanted to escape.

He said To the right of them.

I looked on the other side of the Bottle Banks and I couldnt see anything just the wall with the concrete posts and the slab that was missing.

He said Theyre all there cant you see them?

I said Who?

He said The club.

I said What club?

He said The Dead Fathers Club.

I made my eyes hurt trying to see but it still looked like there was no one there.

I came out of the curtain and said Whats the Dead Fathers Club?

I asked the question too loud because I heard Mum roll over in the next room because she still wasnt sleeping and she said Philip?

I said Yes?

She said What are you doing?

I looked at Dads Ghost and he had his finger on his lips and he was shaking his head.

Dads Ghost said Mum cant know any of this.

I said nothing.

Mum said Try and get some sleep.

I said Yes.

And then Mum said Night.

And I said Night.

And I didnt say anything else I just listened to Dads Ghost tell me about the Dead Fathers Club.

The Dead Fathers Club are ghosts of Dads in Newark who meet near the Pub because most of them went there because it is the oldest Pub in town.

They dont meet inside because ghosts flicker out more easily inside than outside and it makes no difference when you are a ghost because you dont feel the cold and your legs dont get tired from standing up.

I said in a whisper so Mum couldnt hear Are there any Romans in the Dead Fathers Club?

Dads Ghost said Romans?

I nodded my head and said Roman soldiers?

He said No but theres a Victorian.

I said Oh.

Victorians werent as good as Romans but Dads Ghost looked sad that I wasnt interested in the Victorian so I said Whats his name?

Dads Ghost said No one knows his name so they just call him the Victorian.

I said Why dont they ask his name?

Dads Ghost said He doesnt speak.

I got into bed and I said Did someone chop out his tongue?

He said No they didnt.

Dads Ghost didnt say anything for a bit he just stood there and I just watched him and I saw my fish tank inside his stomach.

Then Dads Ghost said The Terrors got to him.

I said The Terrors?

Dads Ghost said They get to every ghost in the end.

I pulled up my duvet and said What are the Terrors?

He then said what the Terrors were and when he told me I felt my blood go cold inside my body and after he told me Dads Ghost flickered out a bit and I saw his face screaming in the flicker but I couldnt hear the scream.

Then he said Most ghosts suffer on their own but its easier if you can talk to others.

I said Is that why theres the club?

And I think he said Yes but I dont know because he flickered out and went into the Terrors and I said Dad? Dad? Dad? but he didnt come back.

Mum said Philip?

I didnt say anything I just went under the duvet but I couldnt get to sleep.

Guppy Number Six

It was early in the morning and I was thinking about what Dads Ghost meant when he said it wasnt an accident. I wanted him to come back and tell me but he didnt. I looked out of the window at the Bottle Banks but he wasnt there and so I just sat on the end of my bed looking at my tropical fish.

I was just thinking it must be weird living in a tank just swimming and waiting for food to drop down. I didnt know if it was nice or not nice being a fish in a tank doing nothing. I thought it must be nice because they dont fight each other they all get on. The Neons and the Guppies and the Mollies and the Angelfish. They never bite each other. I kept looking and I thought something was wrong something was weird and I counted the Guppies one

two

three

five

four

and I kept looking for another big tail but it wasnt there so I lifted up the lid and felt the warmness of the water on my face. I saw the Guppy upside down on the water and it was white. That is what happens when Guppies die. The colour goes out of them so they are just bodies just white bodies. And the other fish were just swimming below not minding that they will one day be upside down and the colour all gone out of them and I asked in my head Where do the colours go? and I didnt know.

I got the net and fished out the Guppy and the net went in the water and the other fish were scared of the net and swam fast away from it and they had to turn round because the tank wasnt a river like the Amazon which is where they are from. I got the Guppy out and let the water drip down like rain like tears and I said Its OK the nets gone.

And all the other fish calmed down now the net was out and went back to normal.

I took the dripping net to the toilet and I pushed the Guppy out of it and flushed the chain and it was free out of its tank going to the river but not the Amazon and I put the net back next to the tank and I sniffed up all my snot and swallowed it. I heard Mum turn over in bed and then one minute later the phone rang and I ran downstairs to answer it in case Mum was asleep.

I picked up the phone and I said Hello.

The woman on the phone said Hello? Hello? Is that Philip?

I knew the voice because it felt like a feather on my neck. It was my History Teacher Mrs Fell.

I said Yes.

It was the first time I had talked to Mrs Fell since the lesson on Family Trees.

She said Hello Philip. Its Mrs Fell. I was just wondering how you are doing?

I lied and I said Im all right.

It felt weird talking to a Teacher on the phone. Even Mrs Fell. It was more weird than talking to Dads Ghost.

She said Everyones thinking of you at school.

And I thought What are they thinking? but I didnt say it and then Mrs Fell said We cant wait to see you.

I didnt know what to say and the only word I had in my head was Yes so I used it.

She said Is your mum there Philip?

I said Yes.

I wanted to say something about Romans but I didnt.

She said in a voice that sounded like it was on tip toes Would she be able to talk?

I said Yes Ill just get her.

Then I said Mum! Mum! Phone!

And Mum got out of bed and walked downstairs with sleepy hair and she said with her eyes Who is it?

I said School.

Mum got the phone and said in her sad voice Hello? Yes yes it is. Yes. No. It has but were getting there. No. It just doesnt seem. No. Yes. Oh yes I think he would. I think he wants to. I think it will do him good. Yes. Definitely. Thank you. Oh thats. Oh. Thank you. Bye.

Mum put the phone down and said out of a yawn She was

just double checking that youre going on the Trip to Hadrians Wall. She thinks it will do you good. I told her you were still going.

I said But

But I couldnt think of anything.

When Mum was in the bathroom getting ready I sat and looked at the five Guppies and then I saw a reflection in the fish tank. It wasnt like a normal reflection it was like a reflection of a reflection and I turned round and it was Dads Ghost and I said Dad? in a loud voice.

He said Quiet.

He put his finger on his lips and then he finished telling me what he had to say.

He told me about a man in the Dead Fathers Club called Ray Goodwin.

Ray Goodwin is the ghost Dads Ghost saw first after he left the car and he is the one who told him about the Dead Fathers Club.

Ray Goodwin was a miner who lost his job and he was murdered 11 years ago the year before Dad bought the Pub and the year I was born.

I said How did he get murdered?

And Dads Ghost waited for a minute like he didnt know the answer and then he said I dont know. Ray talks about everything but not that.

I wondered why Dads Ghost was telling me about Ray Goodwin but then he said Ray Goodwin was the one who told him the truth about ghosts.

THE TRUTH ABOUT GHOSTS

1. The only people who end up ghosts are MURDERED.

2. Some ghosts like Dad dont know they are murdered until after they die but they always find out.

3. All ghosts get the Terrors.

4. The Terrors can only stop when ghosts stop being ghosts.

5. Ghosts can only stop being ghosts when they get Revenge.

6. Ghosts can only get their Revenge when the murderer is killed.

7. Not all the Living can see ghosts only some of the Living and they are mostly the children of the ghosts.

8. If the Living dont take Revenge in the No Time the ghosts stay ghosts for ever.

Uncle Alan Is Dangerous

I didnt say anything because I didnt understand. I just stared right through Dads Ghost and watched the black Mollies and the five Guppies in the fish tank swimming together like a cloud.

He said All ghosts were murdered.

I heard Mum get out of the shower and she said Philip? Are you all right? Philip?

And Dads Ghost said Say yes Philip.

I said Yes in a loud voice.

Then Dads Ghost said I have to tell you Philip. I have to tell you because you are the only one who can see me.

I said in a whisper On the news no one was there.

He shook his head and said They werent.

Then he said The brakes on the car didnt work. I pressed down and it was just air.

And I said Oh.

And he said Someone did it. Someone broke the brakes on purpose Philip. Someone who knows a lot about cars.

The words went into my head two times. The first time they were just words and the second time was after Dads Ghost had said them and they went one sound at a time

some

one

who

knows

a

lot

a

bout

cars

The last word sounded louder like it had capital letters like CARS.

And then he said what I was thinking just at the same time as I was thinking it so at first I thought the voice was in my head and he said It was your uncle Alan.

And I said No.

Then he said He wants this place. He wants your mum. He was always jealous.

And I said No.

And Dads Ghost said I have seen him. I have seen him Philip. I have seen him saying sorry. Saying SORRY Philip. I have seen him drive over the bridge looking for signs. I know it was him Philip.

And then he looked at me and said it again.

I know it was him.

You have to trust me.

I know it was him.

And I said No no no.

He said Uncle Alan is dangerous. He will kill anyone who stands in his way Philip. That includes you Philip. And what happens when he gets bored of Mum? He will kill her too Philip.

The words were squashing on my chest and I had to think of my breathing to get the air inside me.

He said You have to stop him Philip.

I said Ill tell the police.

He said You cant tell the police Philip theres no evidence.

I said But youve seen him.

He said Ghosts dont count as evidence.

I said Ill tell Mum.

He looked really angry and said You cant tell Mum anything Philip. It will put you both in more danger.

I said Ill tell him to leave us alone.

He said No Philip no. He wont listen to you.

I said What shall I do?

He stood there and his face didnt move for ages like he was a see through photo and then he said in a voice that squeezed my chest even harder You must kill him Philip.

You must get my Revenge.

The Hole in the Wall

After Dads Ghost had gone I went downstairs and I went to the bookshelf in the office and got the book called Murder Most Foul. When I came out of the office Mum was on the stairs and she had all her Make Up on and her tight jeans and her white top with the little crocodile on it and she said Whats that behind your back?

I said Its a book on Romans.

She clapped her hands and said in her Pulling Herself Together voice Well come on youve got to get up. Weve got to get you some money for Hadrians Wall.

I went upstairs and hid the book under the bed and then I got ready.

When we got to the Hole in the Wall she typed the numbers and made a noise and typed the numbers again and made another noise and then she typed the numbers again and said No.

I looked at her and she said in a whisper voice No. Why? No.

And we went inside the bank and stood in the line and waited and a big fatso woman came and said Is anyone paying in a cheque?

Mum said No but the machines just swallowed my card.

The big fatso woman said Youll have to go to the Enquiry Desk.

Mum said Money went in three days ago theres nothing wrong with the card.

The big fatso woman said Theyll be able to help you at the Enquiry Desk.

Mum said It normally clears straight away.

The big fatso woman said The Enquiry Desk is just over there.

She pointed to the Enquiry Desk and me and Mum went to a sign that was like a big black lollipop and we waited behind it and we waited a long time because an old man in an old man coat was getting cross with a woman who was nodding at the old man and saying things that made him more cross.

And I looked round at all of the people and all of the people looked very sad except the people behind the desk and the people in the banks posters and the banks leaflets. All the poster people looked very happy and they all smiled and they had all white behind them like they were in Heaven.

Mum got to the woman with the big smile and robot eyes behind the desk and said The machines just swallowed my card. I dont know why its

The woman said Right is this your bank?

Mum said Yes I was trying to get money out of my

The woman had a name badge that said Janice Greenfield. She said Right if I can take some details Ill check it on the computer.

Janice Greenfield asked questions and Mum said her answers.

Janice Greenfield said Carol Noble right? Mrs?

Mum said Yes.

Janice Greenfield smiled and typed on the computer and said Right yes youre actually over your limit.

Mum said No I cant be no I

Janice Greenfield said Right according to the computer youve made a number of payments over your limit.

Mum said Money went in yesterday.

Janice Greenfield said Right.

She typed more things on the computer and said Right. Yes its here. But it still doesnt cover the payments.

And Mum looked behind her at the line of sad people and then said to Janice Greenfield in a quiet voice How can I get my card back? I need it today.

Janice Greenfield said Right well Ill see if we can squeeze you in with a Customer Advisor.

And she looked in a big book and she nodded into the book and then smiled at Mum and said Yes if youd just like to follow me Mrs Noble.

And we followed Janice Greenfield to some chairs and she went and then a man in glasses and weird shoulders came out of a door and said Mrs Noble and Mum went in the room and I was left on my own on the chair.

And then Dads Ghost flickered on right in front of me in the bank and he said There is not much time.

I said For what?

He said To kill Uncle Alan.

I said Why?

He said Every year of my life becomes a day.

I said What?

A man with a briefcase and a long umbrella like a sword walked through Dads Ghost and he looked at me like I was mad and then he went outside.

Dads Ghost said This is the No Time.

I said Whats the No Time?

He said The period when Revenge must be taken.

I said What if it isnt taken?

He said My spirit will never rest and I will always suffer the Terrors. Ray Goodwin says they get worse until every ghost ends up as quiet as the Victorian. Ray tried to escape the Terrors but he couldnt. No one could see him. Not even his daughter. But Ive got you Philip. You can help me escape Philip. Youve got to help me Rest In Peace.

I didnt want Dad to suffer the Terrors so I said How long is the No Time?

He said It lasts until my next birthday.

Dads Birthday was December the 10th. It was September the 25th today.

Dads Ghost said Youve got 11 weeks Philip.

I did a sum in my head and said 77 days.

Dad said Yes.

I said Im going to Hadrians Wall.

He nodded and said You must go. You must act as if everything is normal or youll place your mum in great danger Philip. You must do it when you come back.

Then he said December the 10th. That is when we run out of time.

I said December the 10th.

Dads Ghost said If you ever loved me Philip. If you ever loved me at all you will let me rest.

I didnt want Dad to feel the Terrors for ever so I said I will.

He said Youre a good son.

And Mum came out of the room and said Philip who on EARTH are you talking to?

Dads Ghost was looking at me and he said Dont tell her Philip she cant know.

I didnt say anything and she looked at my face and saw something in it that made her not cross with me and she walked out and I walked out with her and she said Stupid bloody bank.

Dads Ghost had flickered out when we got to the Ka car and Mum had sort of flickered out because she wasnt saying anything. She drove the wrong way and I wondered where we were going and then we parked outside of Uncle Alans Garage.

Uncle Alan owns the Garage with another man who is called Mr Fairview. Mr Fairview is a Bible Basher but Mr Fairview never goes to the Garage because he is not a MECHANIC like Uncle Alan.

Uncle Alan has got a lot of money and so has Mr Fairview and when you have a lot of money you are friends with other people with lots of money like in a club.

Uncle Alan once wanted to give Dad some money to get half of the Castle but Dad said No and Mum and Dad rowed and Mum smashed the blue and white salad bowl they got on holiday in Majorca. That was the holiday we went in a Glass Bottom Boat and saw the fish under water.

Mum looked in the mirror in the car and said I wont be a minute Philip.

I was scared of Mum seeing Uncle Alan because he was a murderer but I tried to act normal like Dads Ghost told me and I said to Mum OK.

Mum likes Uncle Alan because he is a Charmer. A Charmer is a type of man that women like and it is men who look in womens eyes and smile with only one half of their mouth normally the right side. A Charmer is normally divorced and Uncle Alan is divorced to a woman called Trisha who isnt murdered. Trisha lives in Devon and Mum says she takes painkillers even when she doesnt have a headache.

Uncle Alan wears a blue uniform and he always has black on his hands from the cars and he is 50 which is older than Dad but he is bigger than Dad because Dad was only medium.

I watched and could see Uncle Alan giving Mum something and I saw another man in a tracksuit who was bent inside an engine.

Mum came out of the Garage after six minutes not one minute and on the way back she gave me the money for Hadrians Wall at the Traffic Lights and she didnt tell me it was from Uncle Alan but I knew it was and I hoped that Dads Ghost wasnt watching me.

Hadrians Wall

Mrs Fell said Many Romans believed that Hadrians Wall was near the end of the world because in those days everybody thought the world was flat and if you went too far you would fall off the edge and die.

Then she said Where you are standing now was the most northern part of the Roman Empire and so it was a very scary place for a lot of the soldiers who worked here.

It was cold and the wind was making whistle sounds like our coats were musical instruments and I think everyone wanted to go back and get warm even Mrs Fell who had an orange coat that said QUIKSILVER but Charlotte Ward had her hand up.

Mrs Fell said Yes Charlotte.

And Charlotte said Were all the soldiers from England or were they from Rome?

Mrs Fells collar on her coat flapped in her face and she put it back and said Most of them came from outside Britain not always Rome but warmer places in the southern parts of the Empire. Imagine what it must have been like! After years spent in warm sunshine having to cross the rough English Channel to a country which was known to be very unfriendly. There was not only the bad weather and the hills but many Britons hated being part of the Roman Empire and would throw stones or vegetables or even spit on the new soldiers.

Right then I felt someone gob on the back of my neck and I touched it with my hand and turned round and saw Dominic Weekly and Jordan Harper laughing at me through closed mouths. Mrs Fell couldnt see them laughing but she could see me turning round.

She said in a soft voice that was very small and quiet in the wind Philip is something the matter?

I said No Miss.

Her curly hair was blowing across her face and she pulled it behind her ears and then she carried on talking.

Dominic said Helmet hows your dad?

Jordan giggled behind me and Dominic kept saying it dead quiet.

Hows your dad?

Hows your dad?

Hows your dad?

Hows your dad?

Mrs Fell said And the soldiers knew that over this wall was not only the end of the world but also some of the most violent tribes they had ever heard of.

I wiped my hand on my jeans and then Charlotte Ward said How long was it Miss?

Hows your dad?

Hows your dad?

Hows your dad?

Hows your dad?

Mrs Fell said The wall went right across the country from east to west and it was 80 miles long and it was 15 feet high which is three times the height of me.

Hows your dad?

Hows your dad?

Hows your dad?

Hows your dad?

Mrs Fell said Dominic is there something you want to share with us?

Dominic said No Miss.

Jordan giggled a fart out of his mouth.

Then Mrs Fell said Where we are now was one of the watch towers. Can you see the stones in the ground curve round? These watch towers were used to send signals up and down the wall if any invaders were coming. Most of the time though the soldiers were not fighting. Most of the time they did more boring jobs like working on repairs or checking who was passing through. Like when you go on holiday and have to show your passport! There were villages nearby and places where the soldiers could eat and drink but it still must have been very hard for them coming to this harsh world away from their families to start again.

this

harsh

world

Charlotte said Would they ever see their families again?

Mrs Fell said Sometimes they saw them again but they had

to serve 25 years in the army and after that some stayed here and some went home but Roman men on average lived until they were 41 and they didnt finish their service until they were at least 43 because the earliest age to join the Roman army was 18 so many of them didnt get the chance to see their families again Charlotte.

And she carried on talking but I wasnt looking I was thinking that 41 was the age Dad was when he died and I thought that was weird.

Where we stayed was in a youth hostel and it was in the middle of nowhere and there were three buildings. One of the buildings was big and that was the main building and that is where we ate. And in that building we had mashed potato which was served out of the biggest pan ever and it tasted DISGUSTING and it had lumps in.

I sat on the table with the Teachers and Mr Rosen said All right Philip?

And I said Yes.

And there were two more buildings and one was nice and it was where the girls slept and some of the boys but the other one was horrible and made out of dark brown wood and it used to be a stables where they used to keep horses and there were eight beds in it and they were bunk beds.

Mrs Fell and Mr Rosen told everyone where they were sleeping and I was sleeping in the stables and I had to sleep above Dominic Weekly. And I couldnt get to sleep for ages and ages and my mind kept moving really fast and I kept seeing different things flashing like photos in my brain. I kept on seeing the circle of stones on the ground and different other things like the field of cows which we passed on the way in the mini bus. And then I kept thinking of Dad and wondered if he was with the Dead Fathers Club or if he was off in the Terrors. I worried about Mum and I hoped Uncle Alan wasnt there and I hoped he wouldnt hurt her.

And then I started to go to sleep but it wasnt like a real sleep. It was somewhere in the middle of being asleep and being awake and after a bit I heard myself talking and I was talking rubbish and very fast and what I was saying was

kelhamisinnewarkkelhamisinnewarkkelhamisinnewark which is a stupid thing to say anyway because Kelham is not in Newark it is two miles away where Dad died. But I was getting louder and even though I could hear myself I couldnt stop because I wasnt properly awake and then I heard really loud laughing and it was Dominic and I woke up then and I was scared because he had heard and he started saying

kelhamisinnewarkkelhamisinnewarkkelhamisinnewark and then other boys were laughing in the dark and there was nothing else in the UNIVERSE just the laughing.

Dominic said Helmets gone Skitso.

Jordan said Skitso Skitso Skitso.

But that wasnt the end because my eyes were heavy even though my brain was moving fast and I went back to sleep but bad sleep and I had nightmares but I dont know what about and when I woke up I was standing on the wooden floor and the window was smashed and there was blood on my hands and I was screaming something and the light was on and the next thing Mr Rosen was holding my shoulders and saying Its all right Philip its all right calm down and I looked round at the faces and all their eyes were scared even Dominic and all the eyes added up and added up inside me and made my legs weak and I fell onto the floor and there was blackness again.

The Disco

The next day Mrs Fell asked me if I wanted to go home. She said she had phoned Mum and Mum was worried but she was leaving it up to Mrs Fell and me.

I said Did Mum want me to come home?

Mrs Fell said with her feather voice and pretty eyes She said if you want to go home you can.

And I wondered if that meant Mum did want me to go home or not.

Mrs Fell said You wont have to sleep in the stables tonight. You can sleep in the other building with Mr Rosen.

And I thought about this and I thought about what would happen if I went home and then went back to school. And I thought about the Roman legionary soldiers going for 25 years without going home and I looked at my hand with the plasters on and the two brown circles of blood like eyes and I thought of Dads Ghost telling me to act normal.

I said to Mrs Fell I will stay.

Mrs Fell smiled at me and touched my shoulder which I liked and she said Well done.

And then she walked away towards the mini bus and her curly hair was blowing sideways.

When I went to join the other boys no one spoke to me apart from Dominic and he kept on calling me Skitso and asking me Where is Kelham?

On one of the mini buses I sat on the front seat next to Mr Rosen who is the Deputy Head and who teaches Geography and Games.

Mr Rosen is a nice Teacher with hairy hands and a good watch but he is strict. He sometimes shouts and gets a big neck like the Incredible Hulk but his neck goes red and a bit blue but not green and when he shouts little bits of spit jump out of his mouth like they are scared of his voice.

But he was being very nice to me and saying There is no shame in walking in your sleep Philip.

He told me about when he was my age and he walked in his sleep into his sisters bedroom and picked up a book and waited by her bed. He said I was dreaming I was in a library.

I laughed but I knew really it wasnt as bad as smashing a window and I think he knew as well.

And then Mr Rosen went quiet and I looked out of the window and there were drops of rain on the glass like little worlds and outside there was grass and rocks and sheep and it was all hills and I wondered if Dads Ghost was here he would be able to see all the ghosts of murdered Romans. And I wondered if Emperor Hadrian was murdered and if he ever comes back to see what is left of the wall and if he gets sad when he sees just lumps of stone in the ground with grass growing over them and a few people walking with maps and looking at them and wanting to go home.

We went to a place with other Roman buildings and they were built in 130 AD which was eight years after when they started building Hadrians Wall which was 122 AD.

We had plans of the buildings and there were kitchens and toilets and bedrooms but you couldnt tell that from the stones in the ground only from the plans. And Mrs Fell and Mr Rosen were talking all about it but I wasnt really listening I was feeling weird like my body was just air and nothing was real and my heart wasnt beating like normal. It wasnt going beatbeat beat-beat beatbeat it was going beat beatbeat beat beatbeatbeat for a little bit which made me think I was going to die but then it stopped doing it so I didnt tell anyone.

At the meal there was black beefburgers which were thin and chewy like shoes and more mashed potato from the big POT.

And then there was a disco which was really just Mrs Fells CD player she had brought from home. She played some music and it was Beyonce and all the girls danced but none of the boys danced except where there was rapping. And Mr Rosen danced like Dad used to which was like a bird which couldnt fly but Mrs Fell could dance well and she was wearing Make Up and green round her eyes which sounds weird but it was nice. I must have been looking a long time because she saw me looking and she waved her arms for me to come and dance and she was dancing with Charlotte Ward and a circle of girls and Mr Rosen so I didnt want to come. But Mrs Fell never stops so she came over and took my hand and pulled me up to dance and Jordan was giggling at me and the giggle spread out like fire to Dominic and even Siraj who used to be my friend before Dad died.

Mrs Fell said Come on Philip. Come and dance.

I said I I I

Mrs Fell said Come on.

And then all the boys were laughing but Mrs Fell couldnt

hear and she took me to the circle of girls dancing and my heart started going funny again. I danced but I didnt want to because it was a girl song about boys and all the boys were staring at me and nudging and my face was burning HOT.

Mrs Fell was only being nice because she thought I was on my own but sometimes being nice is as bad as being horrible. And so I danced without moving very much just my arms a little bit and it was bad and I just kept seeing the faces of everyone and Mr Rosen was flapping his wings and smiling at me and I wished he was cross with me and didnt give me special treatment.

Mr Rosen said All right Philip?

I said Yes.

And after 100 minutes the song ended and I sat down near the boys but not with them. A song came on which I used to like before Dad died and it sounded horrible and stupid now like robots. And when it was on Dominic and Jamie Western and Jordan did a press up competition and Dominic won.

I looked at Mrs Fell and I think I had upset her because she was dancing the same but not smiling now and I felt bad for upsetting her.

After the Disco

After the disco it was bedtime and I went out and ran in the rain to the stables with Mr Rosen. Mr Rosen got my bag which was very HEAVY and we ran to the building where I was sleeping.

I was sleeping in the same room as Mr Rosen and Mrs Fell was in the next room. I heard her feet on the floor and I heard her take her clothes off. As soon as I was in bed I pretended to be asleep so I didnt have to talk to Mr Rosen but when he was getting ready I opened my eyes very very thin and I saw Mr Rosens back and it was hairy like Wolverine and I wondered if I was ever going to have a hairy back like that and I hoped so.

Mr Rosen put his clothes on a chair and he was very quiet trying not to wake me up even though I was not asleep and I thought he was nice for that and I watched him get into his bed and I thought Teachers are just normal people really.

And he went to sleep very quickly and he snored but not like a normal snore. It was like a door when it creaks open and I just listened to him go quiet creak quiet creak and I tried not to think bad things but it was very dark. It was so dark the blackness felt bright like when it is so quiet the quietness feels loud but it wasnt quiet because of the rain and the wind and Mr Rosen.

And then I waited for a long time. It might have been two hours or five minutes because in the dark time is different. And then Dads Ghost came and saw me.

Dads Ghost came through the door but the door was black so it looked like he came out of nothing just shapes like light that grew and made him.

He walked forward and he had his finger on his lips and his T shirt still said King of the CASTLE. And I wanted to ask him How did you get here? but his finger was telling me to be quiet because of Mr Rosen. But he must have seen the question on my face because he said Ray Goodwin told me how to fly.

And then he said Im here because of Mum.

I said What do you mean? Is it Uncle Alan?

And he put his finger to his lips and checked to see if Mr Rosen was still creaking and he was so he said Mum is going to be in a lot of trouble tonight.

Then he said You have to go and tell her to get out of the Pub because there is going to be trouble in four hours time. You have to phone her.

And before I had time to say I dont have a phone he said Mr Rosens phone is right there by his bed. You can take it and phone from the toilets. You have to phone and tell her to stay with Renuka.

I thought this was stupid because Mum wouldnt believe me anyway and I couldnt steal Mr Rosens phone but Dads Ghost said Mums life is in danger Philip. This is very important.

And he said life like LIFE and I thought if it was true I could lose Mum as well and I preferred Dad when he was Dad not a ghost and I didnt want Mum to be a ghost so I pulled back my covers very quietly and tip toed to the place where Dads Ghost was pointing and I picked up the phone.

Mr Rosen stopped snoring and starting making eating sounds click click click.

I froze still and held my breath with the phone in my hand and waited for him to roll over and back to snoring sleep.

Then I followed Dads Ghost through the dark and tried to step on the floor every time Mr Rosen snored so he didnt hear me and I got to the door and opened it as small as possible because it was letting light get in and I slid through and shut it click.

And I went down the corridor and Dads Ghost was there and more pale now he was in the light. I tip toed past Mrs Fells room and where Charlotte Ward and all the girls were sleeping. The walls were white and the carpet was blue and like Brillo Pads under my feet. I went into the toilets and there was water on the floor and I hoped it was water on the floor and Dads Ghost said Philip youve got to call her. Youve got to tell her to get out of the Pub. Some people are going to come. Bad people.

I started to press the numbers 01636 and I asked Dad What should I say?

And he said Anything just make her get out.

I dialled the rest of the number 366520 and there was a click and my heart was going beatbeatbeat.

It started to ring and Dads Ghost said Whats happening?

And I said Its ringing.

And it rang three times and then there was another click and it was Mum sounding posh like when she talks to Teachers saying You have reached the Noble residence. No one is able to take your call at the moment. Please leave your message after the tone.

And there was a beeeep and I said Mum are you there? Mum its me are you there? Youve got to get out of the house because I know something is going to happen. Something really bad.

And then Dad said Try the other number.

I said What number?

He said For the bar.

So I called the bar number. And when the phone was ringing I heard feet outside and I put the phone in my pyjama pocket but it was girl feet going to the other toilets.

And I picked the phone back out of my pocket and it was Dads voice Dads real voice not his ghost voice and it was saying Hello. This is the Castle and Falcon. Nottinghamshires home for REAL Ale. We are closed right now so please leave your message after the beep.

beeeep

Mum must have forgot to change the message. It felt weird listening to Dads voice in front of his ghost and I forgot to speak but then Dads Ghost nodded and I knew what the nod meant so I said in a loud quiet voice Mum. Mum. Can you hear me? Mum. Mum. Its me. Youve got to go to Renukas tonight because something bad is going to happen in the Pub. Mum. Wake up. Please wake up.

And I kept talking but Mum didnt wake up and I went

quiet when I heard the chain flush next door and girl feet go by the door again.

And I looked at Dads Ghost and said in a whisper What should I do?

And I worried he was going to flicker out but he wasnt flickering at all.

The Mini Bus

Dads Ghost looked at me with the most serious face I had ever seen like Norman Osborn in the first Spiderman when he has the nerve gas before he becomes the Green Goblin and he said By his phone were some keys.

And I said What?

He said By Mr Rosens phone there were some keys. They will be the keys to one of the mini buses.

My face was now even more serious than Dads Ghosts face because I was very scared about what he was about to say and about what I was going to say and it was one of those times when you know the words before you say them but you say them anyway as if you are reading from a book and they went like this.

He said You have to take the keys.

I said Why?

He said You have to drive the mini bus.

I said I cant.

He said I will teach you. I will tell you what to do. You have driven before. Remember I showed you in the car park in Mums Ka car.

I said Thats a small car not like a mini bus and I only did it for ten minutes and I was rubbish and this is stealing and Ill be in trouble.

He said Sometimes you have to do something that is wrong to do something bigger that is right. Mum is in a lot of trouble tonight Philip. A lot of trouble. Some men are coming to the Pub later tonight Philip. Theyve got baseball bats and one of them has got a gun. Youve got to get to Mum and make her safe.

I said I wont have time.

And he said You will have time. They are coming to the Pub at half past four when all the streets are quiet. It is only midnight and a three hour drive if we go fast.

And I thought of other things I could do like tell a Teacher but they wouldnt believe me or phone Renuka or Nan but I didnt have their numbers. I could have phoned 118 118 for Renukas number but she is X Direct because of the bad phone calls and I couldnt remember Nans address. Dads Ghost was mind reading because he said Theres no other way.

I went back down the corridor.

The quiet was screaming and I got to the door and I pressed down the handle and held my breath like I was going underwater. I opened the door and closed it but not all the way and Dads Ghost went through me and in front and pointed at the floor where the keys were. Mr Rosen was snoring and I bent and didnt breathe and my hand went low and touched the carpet and then I moved my hand like a SPIDER and touched cold metal and picked them up in a tight fist clink and I stood up and started to walk out still dark underwater and Mr Rosen turned over and said my name like a question Philip? and I looked at Dads Ghost and Dads Ghost said Tell him youre going to the toilet and I said Im going to the toilet and Mr Rosen made a noise which was like OK but he was falling back to sleep and Dads Ghost pointed to my shoes and my jumper on the floor and I picked them up and I kept going and out and shut the door click.

We went back down the corridor fast and quietly on the Brillo Pads and one of my shoes was wanting to escape and not steal the mini bus and was coming out of my arms. I walked really fast past Mrs Fells room and the toilets and the girls room but at the end of the corridor the shoe dropped clump on the floor. I picked it up and pushed the door at the end which had glass like Maths books and then I turned right past the posters about Hadrians Wall and Housesteads and the fire alarm and got to the other door which had a special handle I had to turn but Dads Ghost just went through.

Outside it was COLD and I sat on the step under the lamp and put my shoes on. They felt weird because I had no socks and I put my jumper on but still felt cold because I had my pyjama bottoms on.

Dads Ghost was halfway to the car park and telling me with his hand to hurry up so I stood and ran and let my feet get louder as we got further away from the building and the light. And then I saw Dads Ghost turn white and turn into a strange shape with lots of straight lines moving in the air and the lines came towards me fast and that is how ghosts fly. And when he got to me he landed and looked like Dads Ghost again and said There are two mini buses.

I said Yes I know.

He said Lets see the keys.

I showed him the keys and he said I think its for the red mini bus not the white one.

And I got to the car park and I couldnt see the red bus because you cant see colours in the dark but I could see white so I went to the other mini bus.

Beatbeatbeat

It was very WINDY now and there were trees near the car park and they were just black shapes like thin necks and round faces with big hair coming out of the ground and the wind was making them shake their heads and their hair like they were saying Dont do it. Dont steal the mini bus.

I looked back at the building and the other building and the stables and I thought of everyone sleeping and I felt sick but I thought of Mum and that was more important. I got to the red mini bus and put the key in the lock and my hands were shaking not just because of the COLD and Dads Ghost was right it was the right key.

I looked up at the sky I dont know why and the clouds were like black smoke but there was a gap and there were some stars like ghosts flying away from Earth and I climbed into the mini bus and the door was heavy and Dads Ghost was already there.

The seat was high and I stretched my legs like I was elastic and my feet could only just reach the pedals. Dads Ghost pointed and he said Thats the clutch and thats the brake and thats the accelerator just like in the Ka.

Then he told me about the gearstick and told me how to use it and that was like the Ka too but VERY HEAVY.

And I said Should I put on the lights?

He said Not until you are on the road away from the buildings.

And I put my seat belt on click but Dads Ghost didnt need one and I wondered if Dads Ghost was having bad memories of the bridge in Kelham but if he was he wasnt saying. I turned the key and the engine started and warm air came in and I started to follow what Dads Ghost said and move the mini bus and steer which was very hard and I couldnt move it much because I am not Dominic and cant even do one press up.

It was like the Chariot Racing in the Circus Maximus when the Roman Slaves died because they couldnt control the four horses.

And when I turned Dads Ghost was shouting saying RIGHT RIGHT RIGHT because the wheels were going on the grass of the car park and nearly down a ditch. And he tried to grab the wheel and forgot he was a ghost and his hand fell through it but I made myself think of Spiderman and I made myself stronger and the mini bus stayed in the car park and then we went out on the road which was like a snake very thin and bendy.

There was a lot of noise and Dads Ghost said Were going too fast for first gear.

It felt like I had gone miles but the hostel was still there right behind us and then we heard a noise like the engine getting louder. That is when Dads Ghost said Oh God.

I said What?

He said Theyre following.

I looked in the mirror and it was the lights from the white mini bus growing very fast behind us and the lights were bright and had rays like Dads Ghost when he flies.

Dads Ghost said Put your foot down quick.

And I put my foot down and the thing like a second hand went up through the numbers 15 20 25 30 and the hedge on the side of the road was blurry but the lights behind were really close now and they were starting to overtake. And when their mini bus was level with ours I could see Mr Rosen and Mrs Fell screaming through the windows and Mr Rosen was driving and Mrs Fell was waving her arms and in her pyjamas and I couldnt hear them but I knew they wanted me to stop and Mrs Fell looked frightened.

And I was looking at their faces and Dads Ghost was saying FASTER and that was when the mini bus went too far left and we were on the side grass but I couldnt get off and everything went shaky and I was bouncing in my seat and Dads Ghost said BRAKE but my foot was bouncing too much. And then we were bucked like the ground was a horse and we tipped but not right over because of the hedge and it scraped the side and then stopped the mini bus with a bump and my head went forward and hurt my neck. I looked to my left and Dads Ghost had gone and I could hear the door open and Mr Rosen going Philip Philip can you hear me?

I could hear him so I turned and saw Mr Rosen opening the door. He climbed in and got me out of the seat belt and said Can you stand up?

I said Yes I think so yes.

I saw Mrs Fell and she was standing on the road in the dark in her pyjamas and over in the fields behind her there were ghosts of Roman soldiers pulling wooden carts full of stones and another ghost with his hands on his hips and his uniform glowing red and gold in the night and a face sad cross like Mr Rosen and a beard and maybe it was Emperor Hadrian and my heart was going like mad beatbeatbeatbeatbeatbeatbeatbeatbeatbeat beatbeatbeatbeatbeatbeatbeatbeatbeatbeatbeatbeatbeatbeat beatbeatbeatbeatbeatbeatbeatbeatbeatbeatbeat

Dad dy

Dad is a weird word if you say it over and over DadaDada DadaDadaDadaDadada it sounds like guns. Mum is weird too. MumuMumuMumuMumu. It looks like moomoomoo like a cow in a baby book. Father is weird Fat her and Mother MOT her and Daddy or Daddie or Dad die

Dad

dy

Dad

dy

Dad

dy

Dad

dy

ing

If you spell Newark new ark which means new work in a different order you get wanker or town you get nowt which means nothing.

Mrs Palefort

Nothing had happened to Mum or the Castle. Dads Ghost had been lying to me and now I was in Big Trouble. I had broken a mini bus and got Mr Rosen and Mrs Fell in Mrs Paleforts bad books.

Mrs Palefort is the Head Teacher and she wanted to see me and Mum when I got back from Hadrians Wall so we went to her office which is on the left when you go into school before you see the corridor which goes past the library and into the main hall where there are assemblies on Mondays and Wednesdays and Fridays.

Mum knocked on the door knock knock and I saw her rings werent on her hand. We waited and Mum looked at me and she had her black Trouser Suit on and her hair back and she closed her eyes and let air out of her nose and behind us there were giggles and stares and cough words burning and burning into me.

We waited and waited behind the brown DOOR and smelt

the sick smell of the clean shiny FLOOR mixing with Mums perfume and then a voice all fuzzy from nowhere said Come in.

Mum nodded for me to open the door so I did and the room peeled open until I could see Mrs Palefort sitting with her worst face EVER with her hands joined togETHER making a church and a steeple but a fallen over church lying sideways on the desk.

Mrs Palefort has dark brown and light white hair in a bun and a big forehead and big square glasses that melt the top half of her face but the bottom half stayed still like it was frozen.

There were two empty seats on the other side of the room and Mrs Palefort nodded her head one millimetre and this meant sit down in them.

Mrs Palefort said Now Im sure I dont have to explain why Ive asked you both to come and see me.

Mum said in her trying to be posh voice No you dont.

And then both Mum and Mrs Palefort looked at me until their eyes had enough power to shake my head. When Mrs Paleforts eyes got what they wanted they turned to Mum and said Do you know how many children in this town are now travelling to state schools outside of Newark?

Mum said No I dont.

1000 was the answer and then Mrs Palefort said Can you imagine what kind of damage an incident like this does to our reputation? Weve got half our catchment area already travelling into Lincolnshire. The best half to be perfectly honest. And we hardly need Year Sevens stealing mini buses on school trips a month before we have an OFSTED inspection. You do understand?

Mum said Yes I do.

Mrs Palefort made a noise then locked her words up in her mouth and went into a long silence like this and then she came out of the silence and said Under normal circumstances we would have no choice but to take Philip out of school either temporarily or permanently.

When she said this Mum started to say something but Mrs Palefort raised her chin like it was climbing over Mums words and said Mrs Noble I understand that these are not normal circumstances and that Philip is still in a state of bereavement for the loss of his father. I also understand that Philip may have been sleep walking or at least not truly aware of what he was doing. This is why he will stay with us for the time being. Under special conditions of course.

Mum lost her posh voice and said Special conditions? What special conditions?

And I didnt hear the first special conditions because I was looking at my bendy shape in one of the trophies on the shelf on the wall. But Mum said later the special conditions were that I had to see the school counsellor once a week but that was all right because the school counsellor was Mrs Fell who is a counsellor as well as a Teacher.

And then I stopped looking at the trophy and I heard Mrs Palefort still talking saying But obviously if these difficulties CONtinue we may have to consider the option of a PUPIL REFERRAL UNIT which could mean taking Philip out of school altogether. But I am sure as time goes by Philip will start to find himself better adjusted to our school environment and I doubt we will see any more incidents involving school mini buses. Dont you Philip?

She wanted a Yes so I gave her one.

Rudyard Kipling

Mrs Fell taught us about the First World War and about a man called Archduke Franz Ferdinand. He got shot and that is how the War started and then millions and millions of men died because of that and that means there are millions and millions of ghosts all over Europe of soldiers and only one ghost of Archduke Ferdinand and I bet the soldier ghosts get cross with him.

Mrs Fell gave us a printed sheet of Facts about the War and at the top of the Facts were some words by a man called Rudyard Kipling who is famous because of The Jungle Book which I watched when I was little but dont watch now because Im too old and because it is on video not DVD and it has Baloo the Bear singing Yes its true I want to be like you who who and the words on the sheet said

'If any question why we died,
Tell them, because our fathers lied.'
    COMMON FORM, 'EPITAPHS OF THE WAR (1914–1918)'
    Rudyard Kipling (1865–1936)

I didnt know what Epitaphs meant or Common Form but I liked the words at the top because my father lied about people coming to the Pub and I didnt die but I did get into BIG TROUBLE. And the words told me that I should tell the truth about Dads Ghost lying and telling me to take the mini bus. Later that day I was with Mrs Fell again and she wasnt my Teacher now she was my counsellor but she looked the same except her head was more sideways when she was my counsellor.

She asked me Why did you do it Philip?

I said Because my father lied.

She said What?

And I said If any question why we died tell them because our fathers lied.

She looked at me for a long while with a very sideways head but she still looked pretty even sideways especially when she crinkled her nose at the same time.

Mrs Fell is the prettiest Teacher because she has green eyes that look into you and black curly hair and a big smile and her top lip is like an M but flatter and her bottom lip is bigger on the left than the right and she wears lipstick but not bright like Mums lipstick and she has white skin that is soft. She wears nice clothes like jeans and a pink T shirt which says ATHLETIC and she has a necklace with a small gold cross like how Jesus died with nails in him. And she is from Ollerton which is near Newark but she does not speak like Nottinghamshire which is sad with the words going

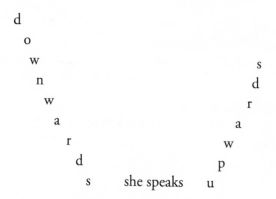

she speaks

with her words not falling even though she is called Mrs Fell. And she just looked at me with sideways eyes the way I look in my tank to see if fish have died.

After a long time she said very quietly as if I had eggshell ears she said Thats from a poem Philip.

I said Yes I know but my dad really did lie to me when I was in Hadrians Wall.

She said You have had a very tough time recently.

And I said Yes my dad died.

She said Yes I know.

I said Its not my dad lying to me.

She smiled and her shoulders dropped down but she stopped smiling when I said Its my dads ghost.

She said Philip when boys your age have to deal with something as terrible and difficult as what you have had to deal with it is possible for them to get slightly confused about some things.

I said He comes to me sometimes and he speaks to me but he is not there all the time. He flickers on and off like a bad light bulb.

She sighed and crinkled her nose again and made her eyes

thin and she said Philip you have an exceptional imagination and that is a good thing to have it really is. But you must be able to separate the things that are real from the things that are not real.

I said Mrs Fell do you believe in ghosts?

Her nose flinched a bit like the question was a ball thrown in her face and she said No I dont.

I said Neither did I until I saw my dads ghost.

She said Philip.

I said Im not making it up.

She said I know youre not Philip. Its just after terrible things happen it is sometimes hard to know what is real and what is not.

I said He told me that Mum was in trouble and I had to steal the mini bus.

She wrote something down on paper and she looked at me for another Long Time and picked up the little gold cross inbetween her thumb and finger and moved it along the necklace. Then she said And when you got back was your Mum in trouble?

I said No.

She said So there you go.

I said He was lying.

She said Philip you have to try to ignore these things because they are part of your imagination.

I said I cant help it.

She said Theres no such word as cant Philip. You have to help it.

I said I have no choice.

She said You always have a choice. Life is full of choices Philip thats all there is. You can ignore anything you choose to ignore and eventually it will go away.

I said What about the soldiers?

She said What soldiers?

I said In the First World War. The ones whose fathers lied.

She said That is different.

I said Why?

She said That is History Philip not Imagination. In fact its a poem so its both.

I said So when I am old and dead and Im in History will I be right?

She said Philip you miss your dad very much. Do you want to talk a bit about that?

I said No.

She said Do you want to talk about your dad? About what he was like?

I said He did funny voices.

Her eyebrows went together like thin caterpillars that wanted to kiss but couldnt and she said Funny voices?

I said Yes. When he bought me a new fish hed do me the voice how the fish speaks like he always gave the Guppies posh voices and the Mollies sounded like this

And I did her the voice of the Mollies and she nearly laughed.

And I told her But his ghost isnt funny hes just sad and angry.

I didnt want to tell her about the Dead Fathers Club or the Terrors. She didnt believe in ghosts so she wasnt going to believe in the Dead Fathers Club or the Terrors. And I wasnt going to tell her about what Dads Ghost said about Uncle Alan because I didnt know if he had lied about that as well and if he hadnt lied she might tell Mum and make Uncle Alan more dangerous.

Mrs Fell said Does your mum know all this?

I said No.

Mrs Fell said What do you think she would think?

think

think

I said That Im stupid.

Mrs Fell said So why did you tell me?

I looked at her arm. It had freckles on it and soft little hairs and I wanted to touch her skin but I didnt.

I said I dont know.

Mrs Fell said You said your dads ghost was angry. What do you think he was angry about?

I thought this was a weird question because Mrs Fell didnt believe in my dads ghost so why did she care about what he was angry about but I didnt tell her the truth I just said I dont know.

Then Mrs Fell asked another weird question which was When did you last see your fathers ghost?

And I said I havent seen him since Hadrians Wall.

She smiled like I had given her the Right Answer.

Angelfish

All fish are the same and no fish are better than other fish really but if there is a best fish it is the Angelfish. The Angelfish I have is six inches big and it has blue and yellow stripes on its body which is round and flat. The proper name for the Angelfish is in my book on tropical fish and it is Holocanthus ciliaris which is Latin like the Romans spoke but the name I call her is Gertie which is short for GERTRUDE which is a funny name.

Angelfish are hard fish to have because they are fussy and have to have water between 80 and 82 degrees FAHRENHEIT for them to stay alive or they melt or freeze. I only have one Angelfish which is bad because Angelfish are better in twos because they have a mate and stay with them for life.

The Angelfish I have is from the

AMAZON RIVER BASIN

in South America which has very warm water like in my tank.

Angelfish come from a family called Chaetodontidae. I dont think fish know they have such long names.

The best thing about Angelfish is that even when they are big they can disappear because they are so flat that when they face you you cant see them even though they are right in front of you.

The Men Who Smashed
the Pub

The noise came into my dream.

In my dream I was playing Football on a hill and I was playing against the whole Football team and I was really good like when I was in Primary School but the pitch was becoming steeper like a hill and every time I kicked the ball it went back into my goal or for a corner and I was losing 20 nil. Dad was referee and I tried to tell him about the pitch being a hill getting steeper but he said Bad footballers blame the pitch Philip. Bad footballers blame the pitch.

And then I heard the school bell in my dream but it wasnt really a school bell and the pitch went very steep like a trap door opening and I fell and landed in bed.

It was still dark and my alarm clock said 04:27 and I heard the noise again. It was downstairs. It was a smash and tinkle noise like someone breaking glass.

I got up and out of bed and out of my room in the dark.

I went downstairs on the bit of the stairs closest to the wall because it doesnt squeak and I walked down and there was another smash noise but it wasnt a window. I waited on the stairs and I didnt know what to do and I saw Dads Ghost for the first time since Hadrians Wall and Dads Ghost said Stop them.

I said How?

He said Scream.

I said I dont want to.

He said Scream.

I said I dont want to.

He said SCREAM.

I said I DONT WANT TO!!!!!!

And the men smashing up the Pub must have heard me because they said something and I saw one of them through the wobbly glass in the door and he was wearing all black even on his face which is called a

balaclava

and then they ran out of the Pub and my body couldnt move not even my fingers and the next thing Mum was behind me at the top of the stairs with her sleepy hair and her hand on the front of her neck and a scared face.

She ran down the stairs past me and past Dads Ghost without noticing him or me and I didnt hear anything for a second and then her voice through the door said Bastards the bastards the fucking bastards.

And then my dads ghost went to be with her and I went too and that is when I saw the Pub.

The Pub was all smashed all the bottles and the door and the till was open and all the money was gone. Mum was sitting under the till on the floor behind the bar.

Dads Ghost was there and he said Tell her to stand up.

I said Why?

Mum didnt notice me talking to no one.

Dads Ghost said Shes going to cut herself on the glass.

I said Mum stand up. Youre going to cut yourself on the glass.

She looked at me as if she hadnt known I was there and then she stood up and she was shaking.

Dads Ghost said Tell her to phone the police.

I said Shall I phone the police?

Mum said No. No. Ill do it.

And she walked between the smashed glass with her bare feet and when she was on the phone Dads Ghost said They must have changed their minds.

I said What?

And he said They must have put it back a month. But it was definitely them Philip.

I said Yes and I said to myself I was going to believe in Dads Ghost from now on.

Barbarism

The next day when I got home Uncle Alan was there putting wood in the smashed window and banging nails.

He said All right son.

The word son itched me inside and I looked at the black on his hands that he never washed off and I thought it will be hard to kill someone with massive hands who hammers in nails really hard. His hands are as big as Queen Angelfish which is the biggest type of Angelfish and too big for my tank.

I went upstairs and Mum was making tea in the kitchen.

I tried to act normal and so I had my book on The Romans in Britain by Graham Fortune but I could only read one sentence. The sentence was

For the Roman soldier Hadrian's Wall was more than just a defence against the Caledonian tribes – it also represented the dividing line between the known world of order and civilisation, and the unknown world of chaos and barbarism.

I didnt know what barbarism meant. It sounded like something to do with haircuts but that didnt sound right. The picture in the book showed the tribes with long messy hair and the Romans with short hair or helmets so maybe barbarism was to do with haircuts.

I couldnt read any more so I fed my fish.

I had just finished feeding them and I was watching the five Guppies and I was watching them come to the surface and take the biggest flakes which are too big for them. Then the Neons below them fed on the bits that dropped out of the Guppies mouths and fell slowly through the water. And I was sitting on the bed and watching the flakes and rubbing the smell of them off on my trousers and I saw Dads Ghost in the glass.

I turned round and he said Hi son.

His face was sadder than it was before and I knew it was because he had spent all the time in the Terrors.

Then he said Im sorry.

I said Why?

He said About the mini bus. About getting the wrong day.

I said Its OK.

He said Your mum wasnt in danger. Even last night you and your mum were safe.

I said The men smashed up the Pub. They could have smashed us up.

He said No. It wasnt his plan. He just wanted to scare you both. He must have sorted the CCTV out. He knew the police wouldnt be able to do anything.

I said There were three men.

He said Yes. But it was one mans idea. He paid the other two. He will probably just add it to their wages. They work for him in the Garage.

I said No.

He said Yes. My brother. My blood.

I said Why?

He said He wants the Pub Philip. He wants your mum. Dads Ghost started to flicker out but I got his last words before he went which he said in his serious ghost voice

fear

brings

him

near

And then Dads Ghost was gone.

Sin

Mum called Alan! Philip! Teas ready!

I didnt want Uncle Alan to stay for tea but I couldnt stop it because Uncle Alan was staying for tea most days now.

Mum had made a chilli sin carne. Mum says chilli sin carne is a chilli without meat and Mums Weight Watchers cookbook says SIN means without in Spanish which is what they speak in Mexico where chilli comes from. And CON means with and carne means meat and she made it with Tofu instead of meat because it has less fat and Uncle Alan was talking non stop just words words words.

You arent SAFE here on your own.

What if it happens again.

Brian would want you to be SAFE.

I could sleep in the spare room.

Dont mind my place I could rent it out.

Get more money.

See theres method in my madness.

Id be an extra pair of hands.

I wont be under your feet.

Im at the Garage most of the hours God sends.

Ill work at the Garage all day and help with the Pub at night.

It would be the easiest thing in the world.

And Dads Ghost was standing by the cooker and watching Uncle Alan do his half smile and his eyes which poured into Mum.

Dads Ghost said to me He sits there smiling. That evil villain sits there smiling. Trying to worm his way in like a maggot. Smiling smiling smiling. Look at him Philip. Look at him. Smiling damned villain.

I looked at him. I looked at his hands with the black on them and they were over Mums hands.

Mum looked at me looking and then looked at my plate and said Arent you going to eat that?

And I said No.

Mum said Philip youll waste away.

And Uncle Alan said Go on Philip do as your mum says. Get it eaten.

And I looked at Dads Ghost and I thought he was going to say dont eat it but he didnt. He said Eat it Philip youll need your strength.

And so I picked up my fork and started to eat and Mum smiled at Uncle Alan thinking he had got me to eat it and that made me so mad and Dads Ghost could see it made me so mad but Mum couldnt see it like my mood was a ghost. She couldnt see it and before I knew what was happening the plate of chilli was flying through Dads Ghost and crashing into the unit door and there was chilli sin carne all over the floor.

That turned the room into a photo. Mum and Uncle Alan

and even Dads Ghost didnt move. They just stood or sat and made their mouths into an O. And I went out of the room and heard Mum say Philip! Philip! Come back!

But I didnt come back. I went into my room and my dads ghost went too.

I shut the bedroom door and Dads Ghost said What are you doing?

I said I hate him.

Dads Ghost said You have to calm down. You have to stay in control.

I said I cant I hate him I cant.

And there was a knock on the door and Mum said Philip?

She opened it and said Philip who on Earth are you talking to?

And Uncle Alan was standing behind her in his blue shirt with the popper buttons and he was looking at me and into me but I didnt let him see the things I knew not like Mum who lets him see everything in her eyes.

And Mum said Philip whats going on? Is this about your father?

And I looked at Dads Ghost and said Dont know.

And she asked me lots of questions and I just kept saying Dont know.

Dont know.

Dont know.

Dont know.

Dont know.

Dont know.

Until she said Fine and went back to the kitchen with Uncle Alan and cleaned up the mess and Dads Ghost went to watch them and I listened at the door and just heard Mumbles but I knew the Mumbles were about me.

And I knew that Uncle Alan was going to stay in the spare room and I knew Mum wanted him to and I knew it was all my fault.

And I couldnt help it. I went out of the bedroom and into the kitchen and Dads Ghost was there shaking his head saying No.

But I couldnt help it and I said Its him its him its him!!!

And I was pointing at Uncle Alan but not looking and my body was shaking and Mum was holding me and spit was out of my mouth hanging and I was in her jumper my face was and I closed my eyes and smelt her warm jumper and it was a nice smell like flowers.

Mr Fairview and the Trout

I was early at school and I got there before almost anyone in my Year apart from Nigel Curtain who lives on a farm 15 miles away and who gets dropped off by his dad on Wednesdays when his dad goes to the Cattle Market.

Before I smashed the window and before I screamed out in my sleep and stole the mini bus Nigel Curtain was the one that got picked on the most because of his school jumpers which his mum makes for him and for his hair which is fuzzy and for the way he talks in a deep voice without moving his mouth as if the words are coming from somewhere else.

But now when the bus arrives and brings everyone from Winthorpe Road and Yorke Drive like Dominic Weekly and Jordan Harper I am left on my own and not even Nigel will talk to me.

And this morning when I saw all the people coming I stood up off the bench and started walking towards the main school building because sometimes I am allowed in early. But when I was halfway someone grabbed my bag which was over my back and pulled me and started spinning me round. I saw someone laughing and I saw his colours his black Adidas jacket and his pink skinny face and his fish eyes and his black hair and it was Jordan Harper so I knew it was Dominic Weekly who had got me. Dominic Weekly is stronger than Jordan and bigger and wants to be in the army and has SAS in big black ink on his rucksack and I was spinning fast now and saying Please.

Jordan was bent laughing and Dominic said Please what?

I said Please stop.

He said OK.

And he let me go and I went flying and landed on my hands and scraped them and they were cut and it burnt and I felt tears in my eyes but stopped them in time and Dominic said Ill give you a spade and you can tell your dad.

He gobbed on me and Jordan was laughing.

And I had my meeting with Mrs Fell but I didnt say about Dominic Weekly or about throwing the chilli sin carne or seeing Dads Ghost again but I did tell her about the Pub being smashed up and that is when she told me I should write everything down.

She said it helps to write everything straight on paper or on computer but she thinks paper is best. I asked her why and she said that when you write with a pen it is like writing with a part of yourself like it is another finger. I liked that and so I said the ink must be like blood and she said it is blue so I must be royal like Prince William.

She said that writing is sometimes easier than speaking even though it takes longer and she said it is easier because you can do it on your own and say things that you are scared to speak unless it was by yourself and if you speak to yourself people think you are mad but if you write the same things they think you are clever.

Mum picked me up from school because it was raining very heavy and Renuka was in the front in her tracksuit and talking at 500 miles an hour and they had been to the gym and I sat in the back and looked at the raindrops swimming together like fish across the window and I was not saying anything because I was right and Uncle Alan was staying with us now in the spare bedroom.

And I thought that was bad but I still had more than one month to kill him before Dad had to suffer the Terrors for ever.

After tea Uncle Alan sat back in Dads chair and swallowed his food and said Its a missed opportunity this place you know?

And Mum didnt know so Uncle Alan said I could help you turn it round I could really.

Mum said What do you mean?

Uncle Alan whistled air out of his hairy nose and then he said Take all those Real Ales.

And Mum said What about them?

Uncle Alan folded his arms still nose whistling and he said Stale flat unprofitable.

Mum said But

Uncle Alan lifted his hand and said I know what youre going to say but the facts speak for themselves. People want lager. They want names they know and prices they can afford.

Mum said But

Uncle Alan said Listen. Im not Bill Gates but I know a thing or two about making a pretty penny.

Mum said But

Uncle Alan said Youve got to let your head rule your heart. Not the other way round. The last thing Brian would want to see is this place going under.

Mum said I know. I know. When you put it like that.

And I said Mum can I go to my room?

Uncle Alan said All Im asking is to give my way a go for a month. Ive got loads of ideas.

I said Mum can I go to my room?

Mum said What Philip?

But my question came into her head and she said Yes of course you can.

I went into my room.

And later Mr Fairview came.

Mr Fairview is Uncle Alans friend and he is his Partner at the Garage but he doesnt work there and doesnt have black on his hands and wears clothes that are out of a time machine and he has hair flat on his head.

Mr Fairview and Uncle Alan have been friends for a long time and they always go fishing together with another man called Terry who I dont know but Uncle Alan takes the mickey out of Mr Fairview behind his back because Mr Fairview is part of the God Squad and talks from the Bible all the time.

He came round to see Uncle Alan and it was seven o clock and I was in my bedroom and Mum came in and said Come and say hello to Mr Fairview.

Really she wanted me to see Leah who is Mr Fairviews daughter and she is a Year Eight and that is a Year above me and I didnt know her but I had seen her in assemblies and she is tall and has long brown hair with bits of red in and a smile that curves down at the ends which is nice.

And when I came into the kitchen and started talking to her Mum and Uncle Alan made wide eyes as if we were boyfriend and girlfriend and Mr Fairview just looked at me with his old long face looking like her grandad not her dad. Mum was wearing lots of Make Up and her eyebrows were thin like lines and then I noticed there was a big silver fish on the unit.

Mum said Look what Mr Fairview brought us Philip.

I looked at the fish and the sad smile.

Mr Fairview said Newark Trout straight out of the Trent. Couldnt get one that size from any fishmonger in town.

Mr Fairview is a man who looks like he was born a man not a boy because his face looks like it was never a boys face and he looks like God made his skin the wrong size for him because it has too many lines and it hangs down off his cheeks like a dog.

The eyes of the dead fish were looking at me and it made me feel weird and I thought I saw the mouth of the fish move and say Fishmonger but I closed my eyes hard shut and opened them and I knew it was my imagination.

fish

mon

ger

And I started talking to Leah again who was looking at me like I was funny and Mum said Why dont you show Leah your room Philip?

Mr Fairview said Go on Lambkin you dont want to be with us boring grown ups.

And so I took her to my room and she said Wow youve got fish!

She bent down and looked at them and her hair nearly touched the floor and she pointed at the Angelfish and said Shes pretty.

I said Shes an Angelfish.

And then she said You stole a mini bus.

And I went red like the mini bus and said Yes.

And she said Thats funny and then she stood up and laughed and fell back on the bed and I sat on the edge of the bed.

And we talked and talked and I talked about what my dad was like and she said her dad was OK but he talks about God too much and thinks he knows everything and likes the sound of his voice and I thought like father like daughter but didnt say it and she talked about school and kept on saying Youre funny when I didnt know I was funny but I quite liked it and then after ages she said Have you ever kissed anyone?

And I said I dont know.

And she said Youre funny.

Then she said Ill show you if you want. Close your eyes.

I said Why?

She said Its what you do when you kiss.

I said OK.

And I closed my eyes and I felt her lips touch mine and it felt weird and we opened and closed mouths like fish and she pulled me off and said Your mouth is moving too fast.

So we did it again. When I kissed her I tried not to think about the Horrible Things about mouths and the one million little creatures that live in mouths and the two pints of spit that a mouth makes every day and my mouth was slower and I thought of Spiderman and Peter Parker kissing Mary Jane and I felt good and I wondered if Mrs Fell kissed like Leah.

And then we stopped kissing and then she said You could be my boyfriend.

And I thought about having to kill Uncle Alan and I said I dont know.

And she said Youre meant to say yes. Its bad not to say yes.

And she looked a bit upset and stuck her lips out and I said Yes.

I thought it was weird that she liked me because most girls dont like me but she was different to most girls in Year Seven and most girls in all Years I think.

She clapped and said Hold my hand.

I said Why?

She said Its what boyfriends and girlfriends do.

I said Why?

She said Youre funny.

And we sat on the end of my bed holding hands and outside my window I could see my dads ghost in the dark and he was talking to someone invisible and he was near the Bottle Banks and so I guessed he was talking to the Dead Fathers Club.

And then Leah said Have you got a pen?

I got my pen which was on my homework and she pulled up her school jumper and she wrote on her arm and what she wrote was LEAH + PHILIP and she did it on my arm as well. And she said from out of nowhere Dominic Weekly is nothing.

I said What?

She said I know he likes to be nasty with you at school but he is nothing. He is scared of me and he wont mess with you again.

And I wondered if Dominic Weekly was really scared of a girl. Even an older girl. And I didnt think so but I looked at Leah and I thought maybe he was and I kept holding her hand.

The Four Layers of the Earth

When Dad died Mum didnt wear her tan or her Make Up but when she started seeing more of Uncle Alan she wore her tan again all over and her Make Up even at breakfast and she went to the gym with Renuka again and when she didnt go to the gym she did the DVD and it was called The Hollywood Workout with Nancy and Bobby.

And I was with her before I went to school and she had her face in the carpet and her arms and legs in the air. Bobby with big muscles was saying This is called the Superman move because with your arms and legs off the floor you can feel like you are flying.

And I said Mum how longs Uncle Alan staying here?

And Mum was coughing into the carpet and saying Hes being very kind Philip.

And that was an answer to a different question so I asked the question again and she said Please Philip Im doing my workout.

All the way to school I was thinking how I was going to kill Uncle Alan because the No Time was getting less and less every day.

When I got to school everyone knew I was Going Out with Leah and she was right Dominic Weekly didnt pick on me and Jordan Harper didnt. Well they laughed at me a bit but that was all. And all Going Out is is holding hands at break and sitting on the bench with Leahs friends who are like Leah but not as pretty and all think Im funny even when Im serious. Especially then. And I think everyone was starting to forget about the mini bus because no one called me Skitso now and boys talked to me again not just Nigel Curtain other boys like the twins Ross and Gary who are Carla the Barmaids sons. Ross and Gary are good at Football and they are exactly the same except Ross has a line in his eyebrow.

I played heads and volleys with them at lunch and Leah watched but I wasnt as good but they didnt laugh too much and Leah didnt laugh at all. Gary let me hear some music on his headphones and it was 50 Cent who is a rapper in New York and you have to nod your head when you listen to him so I nodded my head.

I didnt see my dads ghost all day so he was either in the Terrors or with the dead fathers talking ghost things and it was the best day at school since he crashed and died in the car. The lessons I had were French and I learnt la bibliotheque is library and la gare is station and we heard a song called Quelle est la date de ton anniversaire? which means When is your birthday? and which is not like 50 Cent. Cent means 100. And then we had Geography with Mr Rosen and I learnt about the four layers of the Earth.

Everything you see is the top layer which is the crust like on bread. Below the crust layer there is bits of melted rock called

Magma and under that is solid rock which is very very hot and the third layer is melted metal and right in the middle is the IN-NER CORE which is solid metal and that is the hottest bit of the Earth. So the crust with all the fields and the seas and the buildings is like Make Up on top of the hot red bubbly rocks and metals under our feet.

I walked home on the Earths Make Up with Leah and she said Lets see your arm.

I said What?

She undid my button and pulled up my shirt to see my arm and it was normal and she showed her arm and it still said LEAH + PHILIP. And she punched me for letting it fade but it was only a joke punch and she told me about her brother called Dane who is 16 and he is big and muscly and has an earring in his eyebrow and a skin head and a green Kappa top. He is in Year Eleven and we met him on the corner of Harcourt Street and he was smoking and squinting his eyes like the smoke hurt inside him and he had his shirt half out and half in.

Leah told Dane to Be nice.

Dane said Do you want to go twos on this?

He held out the cigarette glowing red like lava and I said No.

He said Dont worry Im only joking.

It went quiet even Leah who speaks a lot normally but not in front of her brother. And in the silence I wondered if Dads Ghost had got it wrong about Uncle Alan killing him because Leah and Dane were nice and that meant Mr Fairview might be nice and Mr Fairview is best friends with Uncle Alan so Uncle Alan might be nice and not a killer. But I thought in my head Dont go soft again.

And Dane said Youre the one who stole the mini bus.

I said Yes.

He said Thats well cool.

And then he said Im sorry about your dad.

I said Its OK.

He said our mum died.

I said Oh.

And then Dane said to me What music do you like?

And I didnt know what to say because I didnt listen to music since Dad died I just watched my fish and did my homework. I used to listen to Dads music which was Marvin Gaye but I remembered just in time and I said 50 Cent.

Dane nodded so it was the Right Answer. And he told me about 50 Cent being shot but still being alive and he told me about other rappers like Eminem who hates his mum and Jay Zee who loves his mum and Can Yay West who he said is good but raps a lot about Jesus.

And we talked and Leah walked behind us and we passed a lot of newspapers in a bush and they were Danes from his Paper Round and then we got near their house and they both went quiet. I thought that it would be a posh house because Mr Fairview was rich and it was a big house but it was crumbly with flaky paint on the door like Carla the Barmaids flaky arm.

Mr Fairview was at the window and pulling back the curtains and staring at me and staring at Leah and staring at Dane. And when Mr Fairview went away Dane flicked his cigarette in the front garden which was very WEEDY and the red bit like Magma landed on the ground but didnt go out.

And Leah said See you tomorrow.

Dane said like in a film Be good to her.

And I said Yes.

Ross and Gary

The twins Ross and Gary were in the Pub sitting down with Tango cans at a table waiting for their mum. Normally they ignore me and I just go upstairs but they were my friends today because they let me listen to their music at lunch break and play heads and volleys.

Ross saw me when I was in the hall and his hand said Come here and then Garys hand said Come here so I went over to them and they said both together All right?

I said All right?

Garys head was leaning to the right and Rosss head was leaning to the left so they looked like there was a mirror in the middle of them apart from the line in Rosss eyebrow.

Gary said It must be well mad living in a Pub.

I said I suppose.

Ross said Do you nick crisps?

I said No.

Gary said If I lived in a Pub Id always nick the crisps.

Ross said Do you nick the peanuts?

I said I dont like peanuts.

Gary said Dont you like peanuts?

I said No.

Ross said Peanuts are mint.

Gary said Peanuts are the best peanuts are.

Ross did a burp in three levels. First quiet then medium then loud. Then Gary did a smaller burp and they laughed and then they looked at me and I swallowed air and tried to burp but I couldnt and then they laughed louder but then they looked at the bar and Carla and Uncle Alan were there and they stopped laughing and smiled at me like they liked me.

Ross said Are you going out with Leah?

Gary said She is well fit.

Ross said Does she have dog breath when you snog her?

I said No.

Gary said Does she stick her tongue in?

I said No.

Ross said Do you get a dong on when she kisses you?

I said I dont know.

Gary gulped his Tango and said Does she fart?

I said No.

Ross said Does she never fart ever?

I said I dont know.

Gary said Girls that fart are gross.

Ross said I hate girls that fart.

Gary said I heard Charlotte Ward fart once.

Ross said Charlotte Ward?

Gary said Yeah it was in Maths.

Ross said Charlotte Ward farted in Maths?

Gary said Yeah.

Ross said I thought Charlotte Ward would never ever fart.

Gary said She did.

Ross said What did it sound like?

Gary said Like just a squeak. Like a mouse.

Gary made a squeak sound.

Ross said Did it smell?

Gary said I was at the back I couldnt smell it.

Ross said I bet it smelt of flowers.

Gary said Jamie Western smelt it.

Ross said What did he say it smelt like?

Gary said Just like a normal one but not as strong.

Ross said to me Have you ever heard Charlotte Ward fart?

I said No.

Gary said Its wrong when girls fart.

Ross said If I was Terry Blair Id ban all girls from farting.

Gary said Me too.

Ross said And from having BO.

Gary said to me Have you smelt Amanda Barnsdale?

I said Yes.

Ross said Shes minging.

Gary said I had to sit next to her on the bus. I held my breath all the way.

Ross said All the way?

Gary said Yep.

Ross said Its 22 minutes all the way.

Gary said Thats how long I held it.

Ross said You held your breath for 22 minutes?

Gary said I had to or Id have got knocked out. You were all right you were on the top deck.

Ross said You can still smell her on the top deck.

Gary said Shes a big sweaty sock.

Ross said Its cos shes ginger.

Gary nodded and looked at his Tango and said Gingers smell more.

Ross said Their farts are different.

Gary said You never hear them but they smell like poison.

Ross said Ginger poison.

Gary said Do you know that?

I said No.

Gary said Its true.

Then Carla was there with her mini skirt on holding her cigarettes which were SUPERKINGS and to Ross and Gary she said Come on you terrors. Home.

And Ross and Gary downed the rest of their Tangos and said See you mate.

I said See you.

And they went and Carla went and I looked at Uncle Alan behind the bar and he went but after they had all gone the word stayed there in the cigarette smoke air Mate Mate Mate and I liked it.

The Good Shepherd

Later on when Mum was working in the Pub I went round to see Leah and I knocked on the door.

Mr Fairview was through the frosted glass fuzzing like a ghost.

He opened the door and he looked down at me with his long old face and twinkleless eyes and in a sad voice he said If it isnt little Philip?

I said Hello is Leah there please?

And he said Yes she is come in.

I went in and it was a weird house a very weird house with pictures of Jesus looking at me and prayers and crosses on the wall and the house smelt like what Mr Davidson the Religion Teacher at school smells of and what the church smells of. It smelt of God which is the smell of old paper.

And we went into the TV room but it was weird because there was no TV and Mr Fairview raised his old hand to an old green Grandad chair and I sat in it and I thought it must be weird for Leah having a dad who is like a grandad and Mr Fairview said to the stairs Lambkin your friends here.

I looked round the room and I looked for clues of Mr Fairviews money which is the only reason Uncle Alan likes him but there were no expensive things. I looked at Mr Fairviews brown trousers and his white shirt which I didnt think you could buy anywhere in town and Mr Fairview said Do you follow the good shepherd Philip?

I said Whos the good shepherd?

Mr Fairview said The great comforter Philip. The great consoler. He who knows and shares our suffering.

I still didnt know the answer so Mr Fairview said The Lord Jesus Christ.

I said Oh.

Mr Fairview said The good shepherd who gave his life for his sheep.

Mr Fairviews face changed into a sheeps face for a second and he said Baaa Baaa and I closed my eyes hard and opened them again and he was back to normal and he said to the stairs Lambkin your friends here.

And this time Leah heard because she said Coming.

Mr Fairview looked at the ceiling as if there were words written on it that only he could see and he read the invisible words and said Jesus said no man comes unto the Father but by me.

And Leah started coming down the stairs in a horse gallop like she was a Knight rescuing me.

Mr Fairview kept looking up and said I am the light of the world he that follows me shall not walk in darkness but shall have the light of Baaa Baaa.

Then all the crosses started to smoke and fire in my mind like the cross that Emperor Constantine saw in the sky before he won a War and made the world go Christian.

Then Leah came into the room and made everything back to normal and she said Dad were going to go upstairs and do some homework now OK?

Her voice was softer and sadder than I had ever heard it and I thought it was funny because Leah pretends to be a hard girl but she is a soft girl really and she even lets her Dad call her Lambkin.

And Mr Fairview said looking into my eyes not the ceiling Yes yes dont let me stop you.

Then he said Better is a poor and wise child than an old and foolish king.

We went upstairs to Leahs bedroom which had posters up and wasnt like the rest of the house. I didnt know where Danes bedroom was.

Leah said Sorry about my dad.

I said Hes nice.

She closed the door and closed the smell of God and said He didnt used to be like this.

I said Didnt he used to believe in God?

She said Not like he does now. Not when Mum was still here.

And I didnt say anything because I didnt think she wanted to talk about it but she kept on talking anyway.

She said Mum died of Cancer she was ill for ages really ill and when she died Dad got drunk all the time and thought me and Dane couldnt tell he used to walk into things and thought we didnt notice but one day he just stopped drinking and got God instead.

I said Does he make you go to church?

She said He used to. Until Dane got picked on at school

about it. He doesnt make us go now. He lets us do what we want really.

I said Dane got picked on?

She said When he was in Year Nine yeah but after a bit he got into fights with anyone who said he was a Bible Basher and they stopped calling him that.

I said Oh.

She said I hate God.

I said What?

She said I hate God.

I said Why?

She said Because he says you cant do things like you cant steal. But he steals. He steals people. He stole Dad and he let Mum die and he saw her in pain and he saw her praying and he didnt do anything. God just looks down at people asking him for help and he doesnt do anything because he knows if they are hurt theyll want to believe in him more and you wouldnt like a person like that so why like him just because hes God?

I said Your dad likes him.

She said He wants to think Mums in Heaven.

I said Do you think that?

She said Sometimes. Do you think your dad is in Heaven?

I said No not yet.

She said What do you mean?

I said Ive got to do something first.

She said What do you mean? Like say prayers or something?

The words were itchy behind my mouth and I wanted to let them out and I wanted to tell her. But I knew she might talk me out of it and I couldnt let Dad have the Terrors for ever so I said Something like that.

She stopped the questions and jumped off her bed and said Wait there.

She came back ten seconds later and she had a cigarette in her hands and I said Where you get that?

She said Its Danes.

Then she held out a clear blue cigarette lighter and she said We can smoke it out the window.

I said We cant.

She said Why? Who says? God?

I said Your dad might find us.

She said So? He wouldnt even notice.

And I wondered if you die when you are 11 and you smoke but Leah was already pulling the window up and the cigarette was in her mouth not lit up and the wind was cold outside cold cold COLD so I kept my coat on and Leah put her coat on with the fur round the hood. She put the hood up so she looked like a kind of animal like something that climbs trees.

And she put the top half of her out of the window and lit the cigarette and from the coldness she said Come on.

So I put the top half of me out of the window as well with my knees on her bed and we looked out at Newark and the church lit up in the dark with its point like a dagger coming out of the Earth from inside.

I looked at the Man in the Moon with his sad face looking down and Leah said Your go.

She gave me the cigarette and I pinched it between my fingers and she laughed and she said Youre funny.

I sucked the brown end and sucked the lava smoke and it tasted of lorries and gardens mixed up. It burnt inside me and it made lots of coughs but when I stopped coughing I sucked it again so Leah didnt think I was a baby. I kept the coughs locked in my mouth and gave the cigarette back and looked at town again and the lights like gold eyes.

Leah said Do you like Newark?

I said I dont know.

I wanted to say more but I was feeling sick.

Leah said When Im old Im going to live in New Zealand where my aunt lives. She lives by the sea.

My skin itched and my smelly tongue itched and the sickness climbed up pushing burps and I said The sea.

And Leah said Dads not took us on holiday since Mum died. The last one we did was Rhodes.

My itchy tongue said I went to Rhodes I went to Rhodes I went with Dad.

Leah looked at me and said Youre a ghost.

I said What?

Leah said Your face is like white.

I said Im not a ghost.

Leah said You going to be sick?

I said No.

Leah said You sure?

I said Yes.

I looked away from the smoke and in the sky I saw white lines flying to me and they stopped and then it was Dads Ghost floating in the air.

He said It is too much Philip. Its too much. Philip the Terrors are too much. You have to help me Philip. You have to help me.

I threw up sweet white sick out of the window and I said with sick strings on my mouth Sorry Im sorry.

She dropped the cigarette a falling red star and said Its OK Ill get some water or something.

The Dog Noises

I woke up in the night and I heard a noise like a dog crying. I lay in bed in the dark and I wondered what the noises were. I listened and there was the bubble of the fish tank and the dog noises coming out of the wall. When I listened hard they sounded like Mum but weird like she was crying backwards.

I looked round the room and Dads Ghost wasnt there and I got out of bed and I looked out of the curtain and Dad wasnt by the Bottle Banks so maybe he was in the Terrors. And I walked past the fish tank and I waited behind my door and I thought What if its Uncle Alan killing Mum like he killed Dad?

I went out of my door and on the landing and the noise was louder and it was Mum. And I looked for a weapon but there was nothing and I went on the carpet and it was very dark and the patterns were moving and my heart was beat beatbeat and I was VERY SCARED.

Mums door was open only a tiny bit and I moved past her door so I could see in through the crack. And on the floor was her bra and the label which said Fortin and through the crack I saw the mirror on the dressing table and all Mums tubs and tans and pots like a city with lots of Skyscrapers. And in the mirror I saw Mum and a man and the man was Uncle Alan and it took me two seconds to work out what it was. In the first second I thought it was Uncle Alan fighting Mum but in the second second I knew he was having sex with her.

They had no clothes on and the light by the bed was on and the shadows were like giant monsters on the wall behind the mirror. They couldnt see me because I was in the dark and Mums eyes were closed and Uncle Alans head was the back of his head. And they had no clothes on and Mum was biting her mouth like she didnt want to make the noises but she was. And one of her hands and her shiny nails were in his back which was fat and her other one was under his big dirty hand and I saw his red bum wobble and her brown legs round him like a hug but with legs not arms. And Mums blonde hair was all out on the bed like she was underwater and that is when I saw Dads Ghost standing over them and watching.

I dont know if he had just flickered on or if hed been there all the time because I was just looking at the bed and not hearing anything just the noises and he was standing there and glowing like a glow worm.

He saw me and said Dont hate her Philip. Dont hate your Mum Philip. She cant see the rotten Cancer she is letting into this place. Its unnatural but she is too weak. He could kill her. He could kill you. It is up to you Philip. It is up to you to Revenge my murder and stop him before he gets any

Dads Ghost stopped because Mum started making bigger noises saying Oh Oh Oh.

Dads Ghost closed his eyes and then said Kill him Philip. Hes a snake. If you ever loved me youll kill him. Because every sound I hear in this room is killing me over and over. Its Hell Philip. Im in Hell.

I thought this was weird because he was acting like it was worse than the Terrors and I thought nothing was worse than the Terrors.

I didnt say anything. I just stood there and Dads Ghost flickered out and I stood there watching Mums mouth get wider and wider and wider and his big hands were grabbing her and then I think Mum opened her eyes just a little bit and I think she could see me but she didnt say anything just Oh Oh Oh.

I stepped back into the dark and back to my room and there was nothing in my head but IF YOU EVER LOVED ME and the dog noises.

When I got into bed I read Mums book that I had kept under the bed since before Hadrians Wall and the book was Murder Most Foul by Horatio Wilson. It is a book of true murders and people who might have been killed.

I stayed awake all night and I read it to see how I was going to kill Uncle Alan. I looked in it and there were lots of stories about different people. There was one about Marvin Gaye and I stopped because Marvin Gaye was Dads favourite singer. Marvin Gaye had a fight with his dad and then Marvin Gayes dad killed him with a gun and he wasnt a rapper so he died straight away.

There were pictures of dead bodies and there was a bit about people who might have died of murder and might not have like Napoleon Bonaparte who was French and might have died of POISON or might have died of Cancer in the stomach like Grandad. There was a man called Edgar Allan Poe like Poo who told stories about ghosts and he might be a ghost but everyone thought he had just got too drunk. And there was Marilyn

Monroe who Mum watched about on TV and Princess Diana who Mum liked as well and a man called Christopher Marlowe who no one knows why he died he might have been a spy.

And the last story in the book was about a woman called LANA TURNER who was a film star in Hollywood ages and ages and ages ago and she won an Oscar which is the top prize and she was beaten up on that night by a gangster man she had sex with. Her child called Cheryl Crane killed the man for RE-VENGE. And I knew what Cheryl Crane would do to Uncle Alan she would kill him right now. She wouldnt wait and shes a girl!

Spiderman 2

In the morning I sat on the toilet. I had been and wiped but I didnt leave the seat. I just sat and watched the dust in the light make a universe with moving stars and planets and gold suns. I sat and stared into Space for I dont know how long not knowing what to do and then after some minutes my dads ghost came through the locked door. He looked at me for a while and didnt say anything. After a bit he said To be or not to be thats the question Philip.

I said What do you mean? and Uncle Alans heavy feet went by the door.

Dads Ghost said You must put an end to this son. There must be an end.

And I said But

But that is all I said because he flickered out. I just sat there a bit more still not flushing the chain and I was smelling my smell and thinking about what Dads Ghost said and what Dads

Ghost meant and I knew he wanted me to kill Uncle Alan very soon and not wait until Dads Birthday.

I tried to think what I should do and I thought what other people would do and not just Cheryl Crane. This is when I thought of where I had seen someone who had to kill someone to get Revenge for their dad and that is when I thought of Spiderman.

Spiderman kills the Green Goblin who is Norman Osborn who is the Dad of Harry Osborn. Harry wants to kill Spiderman and get Revenge. But Spiderman is really Peter Parker and Peter Parker is Harrys best friend. In Spiderman 2 Harry finds out that Peter Parker is Spiderman. He doesnt know what to do but then he sees his dads ghost in a mirror telling him to Kill Spiderman. Then Harry smashes the mirror and he finds the Green Goblin costume and everything and in the Spiderman comics Harry becomes the second Green Goblin and plans to get his Revenge.

But Spiderman is a bit different to my problem. I dont have special powers like the Green Goblin and also Harry is cross with Peter Parker not just because of his dad but because of Mary Jane. Mary Jane is very pretty and she was Harrys girlfriend. But then Peter Parker made her his girlfriend and Harry said he was OK but he wasnt really because he still fancied Mary Jane.

And this is different to me and Uncle Alan because Uncle Alan hasnt pinched Leah he has pinched my mum. I dont fancy my mum even though she is pretty because if you fancy your mum it is DISGUSTING!

I got off the toilet and I flushed the chain and washed my hands and went back out and in the hallway I saw Uncle Alan and he made me jump out of myself and back in. And he was pretending to leave the Spare Bedroom but I had just heard his big feet leave Mums bedroom and Mum was nowhere still in bed.

He said Morning Philip.

He had his dressing gown open and on his T Shirt was the Cross of Saint George and it said ENGLAND GLORY.

I said nothing.

He said Morning Uncle Alan like that was what he wanted me to say but I didnt say anything.

I just went past him and his big hand went on my shoulder and the hand froze my body.

He said Youre going to be a good lad arent you Philip? Youre going to be a good lad and make sure you make your mum happy?

In an invisible ice cube out of my mouth I said Yes.

He said Good.

The Hungry School

I looked at the butter. It had bits in because Uncle Alan left bits everywhere. He didnt wipe his knife and Mum used to mind it when Dad left bits in the butter or in the jam but she didnt mind Uncle Alans bits. I kept making eyes to the bits when Mum was looking at me but she didnt say anything.

He scraped his toast and the noise went all through me like a rough hairbrush and he said with a mouth of wet toast Arent we lucky Philip?

My eyebrows said Why?

Uncle Alan said Most men have to have breakfast with a badgers behind every morning and weve got this fine oil painting to look at.

I said Mums not a painting.

Uncle Alans toast was all mushy in his mouth in 1000 bits and he said Its a figure of speech Philip. A figure of speech.

He slurped his tea and I felt sick thinking about the toast

and the tea in his mouth at the same time and Mum said If Im a painting Im one of those Picassio wotsits.

And she laughed.

Uncle Alan said One of those eye on the cheek jobbies.

And he laughed too.

Rain slapped on the window like it didnt like the joke and Mum said Oh Philip you cant walk round to school in this.

I said I can.

And Uncle Alan said Why dont I take him on my way round to the Garage?

And I had 75 answers in my head and answer one was Because you are a murderer who wants to kill me like you killed my dad and I dont know how to kill you yet.

Mum said What a good idea!

I said Its all right Ive got a hood.

The rain whooshed against the window and Uncle Alan said No ILL take you youll drown out there lad.

His eyes had mouth locks in them so I couldnt speak.

He finished his toast and he finished his tea and he went to get his blue overalls and Mum looked at me and smiled and in a whisper she said Thanks.

I said What for?

She said For making an effort with Alan.

I said Hes Uncle Alan.

She said Its very good of you Philip. Youre being very strong.

I said I want to walk to school.

She said Now come on. Its far too miserable. Right do you want to give me a hand putting all this in the dishwasher?

I looked at Mums neck and Mums face and I said Why are you so brown?

She said What do you mean Philip?

I said Your face. Your neck. Your arms.

She said Its only a bit of St Tropez.

I said Is it for him?

She said No. No its not you cheeky thing. Its for me.

I said Why? And why does he leave that there?

I pointed to his fishing rod leaning against the fridge.

She said Youre just one big question mark sometimes Philip honestly.

I said Do you love him?

In a whisper voice she wanted me to catch she said Philip.

I said Hes going to stay here now for ever isnt he?

She said Philip stop it.

I said What about Dad?

She said Philip please.

Uncle Alan the big blue giant came in the room and broke the thought with flying high eyebrows and he said Right lets go.

He smiled the Show Mum Smile that straightened Mums back and made her lift her chin like a cat.

And he went over and kissed her cheek and patted her bum and this was Uncle Alan saying he was the new King of the Castle.

He said Ill be back a bit late tonight.

Mum looked at me with scared eyes and the look said Uncle Alan was here for ever and she said Right OK.

I followed the big blue giant downstairs thinking I can kill him I can kill him. We went outside in the rain and he beeped the locks and I got in and hated the wet feeling in the dry car and I wished Id just walked in the rain and then Uncle Alan was there next to me moving his seat back and the rain on his face running down like tears.

He twisted his key and woke up the car and he said The thing about cars Philip theyre like people. Theyve got different personalities and this ones a grumpy old bugger who aint too perky in the mornings.

And I thought Dont try and be nice dont try and be nice.

He switched on the heater and the windscreen wipers that couldnt catch up with the rain and he looked out for traffic leaning forward and squinting. He said Youre not sure about me are you Philip?

I said What?

He said Youve got your doubts.

He pulled out on the road.

I said nothing.

He said Im not your dad Philip. I never will be.

I said nothing.

He said I just care a lot about your mum. About both of you.

Rain wipers rain wipers rain.

He said I know you want whats best for her and so do I.

Words water words water words.

He said Im not pretending its easy for you.

Dad killer Pub smasher Mum fucker.

He said Nearly there.

I said Just drop us off here.

He said I can take you to the gates.

I said Its all right.

He said Youll get drenched lad.

I said Its all right.

He said Ill take you to the gates.

I said I can get out here.

He said Its only round the blooming corner.

I said I want to get out.

He said Jesus.

He stopped the car in the road with another car behind

beeping and I did my seat belt and got out and I said Bye and he said Bye like an echo and he drove off watching me and I turned the corner and there was school and I made my steps last because it was Rugby today. So I let the rain drum its tune on my coat as the others ran past me over the road to the school gates with bars like teeth ready to eat another day out of them and out of me.

100 Miles

At break it wasnt raining any more so we sat on the wet grass by the fence at the back of the field 100 miles from school. The noises of the boys playing Football were far away like birds and Leah was pulling the grass out of the ground like hair so the earth was getting browner and less green. I told her about Mum and Uncle Alan having sex and she said Thats gross.

I thought of having to kill Uncle Alan and I said Will you run away with me?

And she said Run away? Are you mental?

I said Will you?

She said Where?

I said Anywhere just somewhere nice.

And she said Where?

I tried to think of places that were nice and I thought of Sunderland which is not nice and places Ive been on holiday like Rhodes and Orlando and Majorca which are nice but abroad and too far and so I said Nottingham.

Leah stopped pulling out the grass for a second and looked at me and said Nottingham?

And I said Or Derby or Lincoln.

She said Nottingham or Derby or Lincoln?

And I said Yeah.

She said Theyre too close. What about Skegness?

But she said it like Skeg nest like Skeg was a bird and we could live in its nest and then she told me about her dads sister who ran away to New Zealand. And how one day she wants to live in New Zealand.

I said So you want to do it?

She didnt say anything for a long long time and she looked sad in her eyes the way she looks when she talks about her dad but after the long time she said No.

I said OK.

And then the bell rang quiet but not quiet enough and we walked back over the field.

Rugby

Dad went to my school when he was young because he did an exam and passed and Uncle Alan did the exam and he failed so he went to thick school and Dad went to clever school called grammar school and clever schools did Rugby and thick schools did Football.

Now our school is not a clever school or a thick school it is both but it still wants to be a clever school and make out it is posh so it still does Rugby to pretend and Rugby is the most stupid sport in the world it is more stupid than Cricket and Rounders.

I was standing on the line by the big H and I was with the other boys in the Games lesson for Rugby and I felt like a Gladiator in the Games in the Colosseum who was going to die.

Mr Rosen was our Games Teacher today and he told Jamie Western and Jordan Harper to pick teams. Jordan Harper looked at the row with his fish eyes and said Dominic and Dominic went over to his team. Then Jamie Western looked at the row with his squinty eyes and said Scott and Scott is massive and Jamies best friend so I knew hed pick him first. Jordan said Luke and that was OK because I knew Jordan wouldnt pick me because he hated me. Jamie Western was at my Primary School and I went to his house once on Beacon Hill and his mum made us Fish Fingers and we had Sunny Delight and he used to like me but now he ignores me. He said Paul and Paul went over to his team.

I looked both sides at who was left in the row and I saw Nigel Curtain in his shorts like a skirt and his Rugby top as tight as his skin tucked high in and his curly hair like a scribble and I said in my head Make Nigel last not me. And I thought maybe because I was going out with Leah I might not be last for once but Rugby was different to the rest of school and it had different rules.

Jordan and Jamie kept calling names.

Jake.

Robbo.

Siraj.

Kirk.

Pick me pick me pick me.

Jay.

Michael.

Shaun.

Make Nigel last make Nigel last.

Tyrone.

Sam.

Jules.

Me me me me me.

Liam.

Daniel.

Not Nigel not Nigel not Nigel.

Benji.

And it was only me and Nigel and Sad Sack left and Sad Sack was Andrew Kingsman who everyone called Sad Sack because he was like a sack full of sad things. And it was Jordans turn to pick and he was laughing and said to Mr Rosen Its all right Sir Western can have them.

And then everyone started laughing at me and Sad Sack and Nigel Curtain and an aeroplane went over the sky and I wanted to be in the aeroplane I didnt mind where it was going.

Mr Rosens neck got angry with Jordan and Mr Rosen said If you want to be in detention till five o clock keep acting the clown boy.

So Jordan said Sad Sa I mean Andrew.

Sad Sack went over and it was only me and Nigel left standing like the soldiers in World War One when they got shot because they didnt want to fight and I sucked air into me and tried to make me look bigger but I looked little like a full stop next to the H.

And Jamie looked at Nigel and he looked at me and then he looked at Nigel and he looked at me and it was like he was looking at the boiled potato and the boiled carrots on his plate after he had the Fish Fingers and I was the boiled carrots.

Jamie said Philip.

And I was happy for five seconds not to be Nigel Curtain and for having Leah as my girlfriend. I walked over to Jamies team and Nigel walked over to Jordans team with his skirt flapping and then we played Rugby. I didnt know the rules I just knew that if you catch the ball everyone jumps on you so you didnt want to catch the ball.

I stayed at the back of the field but Mr Rosen shouted at me Philip get in the game boy. Get in the game.

So I ran a bit and Jamie had the ball and everyone was coming at him so he turned round and he couldnt see any of his team only me so he threw it at me and it hit my face but I caught it and the ball turned me into a magnet and the whole field was coming to me.

I saw him on the field. He was behind all the running boys and I didnt move I was just a statue holding the ball looking at Dads Ghost.

And someone grabbed my legs and I was run over by about ten boys and they were all on top of me and it was black and I felt my bones squeezing.

Rugby is weird because it lets people hurt you and jump on you on the field and if they did it 30 minutes before at break theyd get told off but in Rugby you are meant to do it.

Its like how in War soldiers are told to kill other men and then they are Heroes but if they killed the same men when they were not in War they are Murderers. But they are still killing the same men who have the same dreams and who chew the same food and hum the same songs when they are happy but if it is called War it is all right because that is the rules of War.

So it is not the thing that is bad or good it is what the thing is called like in Roman times when the Emperors let people watch the Games in the Colosseum where Slaves killed each other and people cheered.

The bodies got off me and I stood up and I didnt have the ball now and Dads Ghost was still there and he said Youve got to play Philip.

I said I cant.

He said Go after the ball son.

My Dad played on the same field when he was 11 and he was good and he was in the team and I wanted to make him pleased with me because I knew he was Cross I hadnt killed Uncle Alan yet.

He said Go on.

I started running towards the ball like all the other boys and Siraj had the ball and everyone was coming at Siraj and grabbing his legs and Siraj was going Raaaaaa and trying to keep going forward.

Dads Ghost said Grab the ball Philip.

I looked at Dads Ghost and he said Take it out of his hands.

I grabbed the ball and Siraj made his hands go tighter on it but I kept pulling it and Siraj didnt care that Leah was my girlfriend and he said Philip get off you wanker.

Dads Ghost said Pull hard Philip pull hard.

I pulled hard while other boys tried to push Siraj down and the ball came slowly out of his hands like an egg out of a hen. It slipped out and it was mine and I didnt know what to do.

Dads Ghost was shouting and waving his arms like a Football Manager and helping me so I would help him Rest In Peace and escape from the Terrors. He was saying Left left.

So I ran left.

Then he said Right right.

I ran right just before Dominic Weekly could tackle me and he landed on his front on the ground and I kept on running and Dads Ghost said Watch out behind you.

I turned and saw Jordan running fast in his Reeboks with his wide fish eyes and his tongue sticking out of the side of his mouth.

Dad said Run Philip run.

So I changed gear and went very fast.

Dad said Left left.

So I moved left and saw Jordans hands just miss my ankles.

Dad said Get past the line son.

So I kept running right through the H and put the ball down on the ground and got the Try and I heard Mr Rosen blow the whistle and I heard cheers in my head. Dads Ghost was nodding like he was proud of me and I kept waiting for everyone to run up and jump on me and say Nice one like they do when anyone else scores a Try but they didnt do anything but furry legs Mr Rosen smiled at me and said Where did that come from?

I said I dont know.

He said Well played Philip you should come to the practice on Thursdays after school.

And he looked at me with eyes that werent cross about the mini bus any more and his hairy hand patted my shoulder when I walked back down the field and I turned to see Dads Ghost but he was gone.

Halloween and the Ra Ra Ghosts and Sleepy Eye Terry

Mum said Philip can you get the door love?

I went downstairs still in my uniform and I opened the door and it was a skeleton and a Green Goblin.

The skeleton said Trick or Treat?

The Green Goblin said Treat or Trick?

I said I dont know.

The skeleton laughed and then the Green Goblin laughed.

The skeleton said Its us you div.

The Green Goblin said Which is which?

The skeleton said Yeah witch is witch?

I pointed to the skeleton and said Gary and then I pointed to the Green Goblin and said Ross.

The skeleton pulled off his skull mask and it was Ross with the line in his eyebrow and he said in a burp Close.

And Gary the Green Goblin said You coming out?

I said I dont know. And then I shouted Mum! Mum! Can I go out Trick or Treating with Ross and Gary?

And Mum came out of the bar drying a glass and Carla was in the Pub working so Mum said OK but no more than an hour.

Her mouth was tight like it wanted to say something else but it didnt.

When we got out of the door the coldness woke me up and I said I dont have a costume.

Gary said Put your tie round your head.

Ross the skeleton said Yeah put your tie round your head.

Gary said Tie it round.

Ross said Yeah tie it round.

I undid my tie and tied it round my head and Gary said Wicked.

We went onto London Road and walked past the posh houses and I said Why arent we knocking on anyones door?

Gary said You just get biscuits round here.

Ross said The Ra Ras dont give you money. They give you biscuits or a piece of cake. And crap biscuits not KitKats or owt.

Gary pointed to a big house on the other side of the road with three levels and tall thin windows and said We knocked on that house last year and some Ra Ra came out and gave us a banana and like a small orange. All happy like it was a tenner.

Ross said So we gave him a Trick anyway.

Gary laughed and shook his head A banana!

We went onto Winchelsea Avenue and there were smaller houses joined together with flat windows and net curtains and we knocked on the first door.

A woman answered. It was a pregnant woman rubbing her big baby bump and Ross and Gary said together Trick or Treat?

And then I said Trick or Treat?

And the woman blew heavy air out and said Not again.

The woman left her door open and went into her house and

we waited on her step and Gary did a two level burp and Ross gave Gary a dead arm and said Shut up you radgey.

Gary gave Ross an even deader arm and the woman came back with her red purse looking in it and then gave us 50p each and she looked at me and my tie and said What are you meant to be?

But I didnt have the words in my head to answer.

Gary said Hes a Zorfmunger.

Ross said Yeah hes a Zorfmunger.

The woman said Whats a Zorfmunger?

Gary said Its a deadly monster.

Ross said If you look into its eyes for five seconds youre dead.

The woman said And er Zorfmungers they wear school ties round their heads?

Gary said Only the chief Zorfmungers. Theyre the worst ones.

Ross said They fry your brains.

The woman kept looking at me and said They dont say much do they.

Gary said They only speak Zorf.

Ross said Its harder than French.

The woman nodded and rubbed her baby lump and said Righto. Glad we cleared that up. Bye boys.

And Gary and Ross said Bye.

And I said Bye not in Zorf.

And then we saw two little ghosts with a man behind them walking down the street.

They werent real ghosts they were just sheets with eye holes with black pen round the holes in a circle and they were Trick or Treaters with their dad and they were on the other side of the road.

And the smaller ghost said to her dad Daddy Daddy please one more.

And the dad said All right one more.

And we watched them go to a house and say Trick or Treat. Even the dad said it.

Ross said in the posh school Ra Ra voice Daddy Daddy please one more.

Gary laughed.

But I was just thinking that my dad never went Trick or Treating with me when I was little because he was always working in the Pub. And I thought about Ross and Garys dad who Ive never seen and who Ross and Gary never see since Carla got a Divorce and stopped falling down the stairs.

And we went to the next house on our side of the road.

Gary knocked in a tune and we waited. While we waited Ross turned to me and said Pull.

I pulled his finger and he farted and then one second later the door opened.

Trick or Treat.

Trick or Treat.

Trick or Treat.

The man was in a bad mood and a tracksuit and he shut the door in our faces and so Gary got out a box from his pocket. A blue box. He took something out. It was something plastic that looked like a needle like for BCG jabs but without the needle bit.

I said Whats that?

And Ross looked at me and said Stink Bomb.

He pointed to the mans letter box and Gary pulled the needle with no needle and it clicked and went longer and then he pushed it through the letter box and Ross said Scarper!

So we ran down the street and Ross and Gary were laughing with their heads back and then we heard a door open and close behind us and then a voice said Oi you little cunts get here.

It was the tracksuit man and I looked back and the street was empty now except the man because the Ra Ra ghosts and their dad had gone. The man in the tracksuit was running after us and getting closer up the street and Ross saw a passage between the houses and he said Down here.

I looked down the passage and in the blackness I saw him. It was Dads Ghost standing at the end as we ran down to him.

He was cross with me I could see in his face and Ross and Gary ran straight through him to the wheelie bins.

Ross said Which gate?

Gary said with his shoulders I dont know.

Ross went to open the left gate and Dads Ghost said No!

So I said No!

Gary said Why?

Dads Ghost said Theres a dog. A Dobermann.

And before I could say it the Dobermann growled and barked behind the gate and so Ross and Gary and me and Dads Ghost went through the other gate and through someone elses back garden.

The tracksuit man was in the passage his voice bouncing off bricks Youre dead you mother Fucks. Youre dead.

We went right through the garden and I felt bad with Dads Ghost watching but I didnt want to get caught and the man was in the garden as well getting closer and there was a wall at the back of the garden and we trod over the flowers which were roses and Ross and Gary were over the wall in one second and I was two seconds because my foot was stuck and Dads Ghost said Quick Philip quick.

I ran through another garden with the man still behind and

Dads Ghost was flying in front and pointing to the gate Ross and Gary had just gone through and I went through it and out on the street. I didnt know where Ross and Gary were they were gone because they were faster than me and Dads Ghost said The park! so I crossed over the road nearly got run over beeep! and got into the park and ran following Dads flying Ghost.

But halfway through the park by the trees the man got me got my back and pulled me and I said Dad!

The man grabbed my neck and pushed me against the tree and said You think its funny now do you?

I said No.

And Dads Ghost said Get off him!

But the man couldnt hear Dads Ghost.

The man had an eye half closed like it wanted to go to sleep and he said I could squeeze the life out of you like squeezing fucking toothpaste.

Dads Ghost was at our side looking at the man and he said I know him Philip I know him.

I looked at Dads Ghost wanting him to do something but he just kept talking.

He said He works for Alan. He works for him. Its one of the BASTARDS who smashed the Pub.

I kept looking at Dads Ghost and the man turned to see but couldnt see him and said What the fuck are you looking at?

Dads Ghost said Whats his name? Whats his name? Whats his name? Whats his name? Terry thats it! Hes called Terry. Philip say Terry. Say Terry Philip.

I had heard of Terry before because Uncle Alan went fishing with him and Mr Fairview.

I said Terry.

It came out as a cough because his hand was too tight on my neck.

His hand let go a bit and he said What?

I said Terry.

Dads Ghost said Tell him you know who he is.

I said I know who you are.

Terry said Oh you do do you you cunt?

Dads Ghost said Say he works for Alan.

I said You work for Alan.

Dads Ghost said Tell him he smashed the Pub.

I said You smashed the Pub.

One of Terrys eyes went wide but the other one stayed nearly asleep.

Terry said What you on about dipshit?

Dads Ghost said Tell him where you live.

I said I live at the Castle. I live with Alan.

Dads Ghost said Tell him youre Brians boy.

I said Im Brians boy.

Terrys hand came off my neck quick when I said that like my neck was too hot like an oven.

And Terry said Brians boy.

But he said it quiet like to himself and he rubbed his hand on his tracksuit.

Dads Ghost leant over and whispered in Terrys ear Now go.

And Sleepy Eye Terry went and I watched him leave the park with my back still against the tree and my tie still round my head and then I turned to Dads Ghost and said Thanks.

But Dads Ghost was gone.

I looked round the park and I could see other ghosts. There was a woman in a black dress holding a candle and a man hanging in a tree and a gold colour dog with blood on his chest and there were lots of ghosts all over but I closed my eyes and opened them again and they were gone like Dad.

PrayStation

When I got back my heart was still beating fast and I was thinking about Sleepy Eye Terrys hand round my neck in the park
but then Mums voice from the Living Room said Philip.

I said What?

She said Come here.

So I went to the Living Room. When I got there there was a
big box on the table and it was in a Dixons bag and Mum was
nodding to it.

Uncle Alan was looking at me and I said Whats that?

Mum was smiling with her chin back in her neck and she
said Its for you. From Uncle Alan. Its why he was a bit late back.
Its what youve wanted.

And Uncle Alan said Something to cheer you up. Stop you
having to gawp at fish all day long.

I walked over to the bag and could see what it was when I
got closer because I could see the words which said PS 2 under
the carrier bag. I got the box out of the bag and I tried to open it

but it was too hard. Uncle Alans hands came from over my head and opened the box and then I got the PlayStation 2 out and it was protected by bubble poppers. It was a grey box with wires and it had instructions and Uncle Alan said Ill set it up for you. I turned to Mum while Uncle Alan was on the floor by the TV with his big bum in the air like he was religious and Mum said with her volume down Say thank you.

Then she said it again SAY THANK YOU like she was shouting but still with no noise like behind a window. And I didnt want to say it because Uncle Alan was only trying to buy me so he could have sex with Mum but Mums eyes were remote controls so I said Thank you but really quiet like Thank you.

Uncle Alan turned round and said What?

I said Thank you for the PlayStation.

He smiled and nodded and said What are Uncles for?

But it was one of those questions with no answer so I didnt.

And I looked at Mum and she was looking at me with a head more sideways than Mrs Fell and she was happy and she went out of the room and Uncle Alans bum was still in the air like he was saying prayers to the TV.

PlayStation

PrayStation

And I was standing there and I was looking at him and then I was looking at the poker by the fire which was not a real fire but it was a real poker. I thought I could pick it up and hit him on the HEAD and he would be dead. I thought of Sleepy Eye Terry and I thought of Dads Ghost in the Terrors and he would tell me to pick up the poker and kill him but then I thought other things. I thought then everyone would know it was me and I would be taken away from Mum and I must think of another way to kill him and not after he has bought a PlayStation.

And Uncle Alan said There should be two games in the box.

And I went to the box and inside there were two games and they were called Primal Curse An Adventure of Fortune Death and Danger and Miami Speedboat 5.

And Mum came in with a glass of Pepsi for me and a glass of whisky for Uncle Alan and put them on the table still smiling out of her neck and Uncle Alan said There you go its all yours.

I put on a game and it was Primal Curse and it was a two player and I sat there with the controls and Mum said Alan will play with you wont you Alan?

And Uncle Alan said Right. Yes.

I didnt want to play with him but I wanted to beat him and his big hands on the small controls and I just sat there on the carpet and he sat on the sofa and we played the game.

Uncle Alan was a man with a sword and a shield and I was a man with a metal ball with spikes and it was on a chain and I could use the controls to swing it above my head and then let the chain go long so it hit Uncle Alans man in the head. Each time I hit him there was a noise like the man was in pain and a blood splat in the air.

Uncle Alan said Ow.

He tried to get his sword out and fight me but I didnt give him a chance and my points and my lifeline went up and his went down from green to brown to red. Uncle Alan just looked at me and I think he was scared about what Id do if I had real weapons and I didnt look at him I just kept pressing my fingers on the controls. That is when Mum came in and said It looks a bit violent.

But I kept going until it said Game Over.

WAYS I CAN KILL UNCLE ALAN

1. Hammer on his head in his sleep. But I will need a big swing and I might miss.

2. Knife in his neck in his sleep. But the blood might go over Mum.

3. Use a pillow on his face in his sleep. But he is too strong and he might escape.

4. Push him in the River Trent which has a strong current and it will pull him to the bottom and he will DROWN in the BROWN water with his fishing rod. But I will need a very long run up and I might fall in and he always goes fishing with Mr Fairview and SLEEPY EYE TERRY!!

5. Wait for him to climb up a long ladder and push the ladder. But I have never seen him go up a ladder.

6. POISON. You can pour poison into someones ear when they sleep and it kills them. But there are no poison shops any more. Weedkiller is poison but I dont know if you can pour it into ears.

7. Carrier bag over his head so he cant breathe. But he would have time to take it off and put it over my head.

8. The Garage is wood outside so I could set it on fire when he is the only one there. But. But. But

The Silent Partner

Later that night I was on the settee writing in my exercise book
Ways I Can Kill Uncle Alan and Mr Fairview was round but not
with Leah and he was talking to Mum and Uncle Alan and he
looked at me and he said Not a titter out of you is there little
Philip?

Uncle Alan said Hes a quiet lad.

Mr Fairview nodded and said Dont worry about being shy.
You know what the Good Book says?

I looked at Mum and Uncle Alan who were talking about
Mr Fairview with their eyes and I said No.

Mr Fairview said The meek shall inherit the Earth.

I said Oh.

Uncle Alan said to Mr Fairview Are you going fishing tomorrow?

I wondered if Sleepy Eye Terry was going fishing with Uncle
Alan as well and I wondered if he was going to tell Uncle Alan
about the park and the Stink Bomb.

Mr Fairview was going to say something but he stopped the words he was going to say and he said I I I dont know.

I looked at Mr Fairview and I didnt understand how Leah is half from him. I wondered what happens in the time between when you are a child and when you are a dad.

Uncle Alan said Its just that me and Terry are going to go down near the weir and see what its like there. Meant to be good Carp.

Mr Fairview said Im Im going to be busy on Saturday. Im helping out at the church. Im in a bit of a hurry actually Alan. I dont suppose Id be able to take those books now.

The books he was talking about werent story books or History or murder books they were blue books with a sticker saying Garage Accounts on them. Uncle Alan gave them over and scratched the back of his head and said Bit of light reading.

Mr Fairview didnt say anything about that he just said Id better get off.

Uncle Alan saw him out and came back in and shrugged his shoulders at Mum and said Hes tapped in the head.

Mum said Id better go down and help behind the bar.

Uncle Alan was shaking his head and looking at the carpet and he said God knows what he wants those books for. He never asks for them.

Mum was doing her lipstick in the mirror over the fire and without moving her mouth she said You trust him dont you?

Uncle Alan said Hes been acting weird lately. Asking weird things. Ever since I wouldnt let him get out of the new contract.

Mum said What sort of weird things?

Uncle Alan sat on the sofa and started reading the Argos book and said I dont know. Just weird things about what hours me and Terry are working. I think he thinks Im spreading myself too thin. What with working here as well. Stuff him. Hes never shown a blind bit of interest before. Hes just taken his share and kept it zipped like Silent Partners are supposed to. I mean thats what it is. SILENT Partner.

Mum put on more lipstick and made her mouth like a fish and said Perhaps you want to keep an eye on him.

Uncle Alan looked up from the Argos book and he looked at me but to Mum he said Someone else is always doing that.

Mum undid a button on her shirt and said What?

Uncle Alan said You dont worry about the God Squad because theyve always got Him Upstairs keeping an eye out. Keeping a score card for Saint Peter. I tell you they knew what they were doing when they invented religion. Its better than CCTV.

Mum said Im going to go down and give them a hand behind the bar. You two boys can stay chinwagging.

I looked at Uncle Alan and he lifted up the Argos book and he said to me You can tell me what you want from Father Christmas.

I didnt want anything from Father Christmas because I didnt believe in Father Christmas but Mum smiled at Uncle Alan like he was being nice and not trying to buy me like I was a Slave on sale in the Forum with a wood sign round my neck saying If you buy me you can do sex with my mum all the time and take over the Pub and be my dad and not my fat red uncle and no one will ever find out you are a killer. A fat red killer.

Mum said Isnt that nice Philip? Philip? Philip? Isnt that nice? Philip?

I said Ive got to do my homework.

Uncle Alan said The Footballs on.

I said I cant.

Uncle Alan said Champions League. The highlights.

I said I cant and I took my exercise book and went to my room and Mum sent a lot of Philips after me Philip Philip Philip but I shut the door and no one opened it.

Not Uncle Alan and not Mum.

Saturday in Boots

It was Saturday morning and I had only got one month and 10 days to kill Uncle Alan if Dads Ghost was going to get out of the Terrors but I still didnt know how I was going to do it.

Dads Ghost said You need to sort it out Philip.

I said Yes.

Dads Ghost said Dont waste time.

I said No.

Mum called up the stairs Philip? Philip?

I said Yes.

She said Leahs here for you.

I looked at Dads Ghost and he was cross with me and said Get rid of her Philip.

I said But

He said I cant take it. I cant take the Terr

But he flickered out and into the Terrors so I went and saw Leah and watched T4 and played Miami Speedboat 5 on the

PlayStation and Leah texted 2000 people and we went into town and she said Lets go shopping.

I thought of Dads Ghost in the Terrors and I said Ive got no money.

She said So? I havent either.

And that worried me and the worry froze my face because she laughed and said Youre funny.

We saw some girls Leah knew and I just stood there not speaking and they went Ah like I was a puppy or a baby not a year younger. Less than a year. Half a year. Why do girls have to make everything sweet? Things are just things. And the girls showed Leah stuff like hair clips and lip gloss which were in bags and some which werent.

And then we were on our own again and I saw Siraj and he was with his mum and he ignored me and then me and Leah went to the Body Shop which is a girls shop. When Leah came out we walked down the street and she said Look.

I looked and it was Peppermint Foot Scrub and she didnt pay for it and when she passed a bin she put it in.

I said Didnt you want it?

She said No.

I said Why did you take it?

And she said See if I could.

I didnt say anything and so she said You do it.

I said What?

She said Dairse you.

She twisted the red bit of her hair round her finger and she made big eyes and a face I liked and didnt like at the same time. Leah was even more scary on Saturdays than on weekdays but it was a nice kind of scary not a Dominic kind of scary.

She said All you have to do is make out youre doing something else like looking at something else then just put it in your pocket.

And I said But its stealing.

She said Youre funny.

I said What if I get caught?

She said Make yourself invisible.

I said What?

She said You only get caught if they see you.

I said I cant make myself invisible.

She said Yes you can. Ive seen you.

And I didnt know what she was talking about because Im not an Angelfish or a ghost that can disappear in front of you.

She said People only see you if they want to see you. Thats how people get caught.

I said What?

Her eyelashes went like butterfly wings and she said If you look like you dont want people to see you theyll see you. Thats how Jenna got caught in Superdrug.

I didnt know who Jenna was but didnt ask.

She said If you nab something youve got to act like you dont mind people looking because then they wont look.

And then she walked into Boots and I followed and tried to be invisible but I felt like everyone was watching me. Even the shampoos were watching me. I didnt know why I was going to take something but I knew I was going to take something so I looked for something small. The smallest thing I saw said Nivea Anti Ageing Eye Cream so I looked at something else Oil of Olay and I put the Eye Cream in my pocket. It wouldnt go in because my jeans were tight and Leah started laughing not an invisible laugh and then it went in my pocket and I wanted to get out but I turned round and I saw hoop earrings and Carla the Barmaid and she said All right Philip? You look like youve seen a ghost.

I said No. I havent. I was just

And I looked at the shelves but Carla ignored me and looked at Leah and smiled tired and said Hello duck.

Leah said Hi.

Carla scratched her neck and said to me Tell your mum Ive got to go to the doctors this afternoon so I might be ten minutes late.

And I said OK.

I had my hand over my pocket and then I said Bye.

She said Bye duck.

And she smiled her shrug shoulder smile pushing the air up and me and Leah watched her leave the shop. Then we started walking and we went out the doors and past the machines and they went BEEPBEEPBEEPBEEPBEEP and Leah said Run.

We ran out the doors out into cold sun and down to the Precinct and I looked behind and there was a Security Guard running and shouting into a black box walkie talkie. The whole town was watching and the Security Guard was fat so we were faster and Leah said Down here.

She went down a black alley that went to the back of the Multi Storey and there were different ways out so we went down a passage with big wheelie bins and hid behind the wheelie bins.

Leah was laughing and she said That was funny.

I was thinking that was lots of things but not funny.

I looked at her face and the red in her hair and her Saturday lips all shiny and we stayed in the wheelie bin shadows in a part of town Id never been which smelt of cabbage and I looked at Leahs eyes and her hair all pretty for me and I loved her because it was the first time I hadnt thought of Dad since he was a ghost like she had gone in my head and shoplifted the sad things without me looking and we stayed there until the Security Guard wasnt coming but even then I didnt want to go.

I walked back through town on my own and I went through the park which is where the castle is. The real castle not the Pub Castle. The real castle is only a wall now and it is the castle where King John was hiding before he died ages and ages ago when he was scared looking from the window like Nan does. I saw Mrs Fell there and she was with a man in a wheelchair and he had a tube on his face up his nose like a straw and Mrs Fell was holding the mans hands and rubbing the top of them and he couldnt move very well. And I watched from behind the bush and I thought the man was old because he had no hair but his clothes were not light brown like old peoples clothes they were red and blue and he had trainers on and he wasnt her grandad or her dad so he might have been her husband but I didnt know.

The Golden House

Uncle Alan came in backwards through the Pub doors and he was pulling a big machine on a trolley.

He said Ah my back! My back! My back!

He left the trolley and he put his hands on his back and scrunched his eyes and another man came through the doors with a clipboard and Uncle Alan signed still holding his back with his other hand.

The clipboard man left and Uncle Alan saw me eating the crisps that I stole and he said Wheres your mum?

I said Upstairs.

He said What do you think of the new machine?

I looked at the machine which was Who Wants to be a Millionaire?

I said Dont know.

But he wasnt listening. He was going upstairs with his bad back saying Carol? Carol?

And Dads Ghost flickered on and he said Philip? Philip? Whats going on?

In my head I remembered a song Dad used to sing.

Whats going on?

Whats going on?

But he wasnt singing now he was looking at the machine and the new beer pumps with lights inside them and the Big Screen and the sign that said Sky Sports 1 2 and 3 and the blackboard that said Karaoke Tonight in green chalk letters that were fat.

He said Where are all my pictures?

None of Dads pictures of the sea and old boats were on the wall now because Uncle Alan says Newarks as far away from the sea as you can get in England. Its bang smack in the centre. It makes no sense to have pictures of the flaming sea on the wall.

I looked at Dads Ghost and said He took them out.

Dads Ghost looked at the sign and said Karaoke?

I said Mum said he could try it tonight to see how it goes.

He said Hes taken the soul out of the place. And hes after her soul as well. He wants to marry her Philip. He might have asked her already. But he definitely wants to marry her. I know it.

I said No.

He said You must stop it happening. You must act fast. You must think of

He started to flicker and do the Silent Scream.

You must act Philip.

You must stop hi

The day went at fast and slow Sunday speed and nothing happened apart from Mum went to Boots and got some Bath Salts for Uncle Alans bad back. When she came home she kept looking at Uncle Alan and smiling like they had a Secret and that made me feel like I was sinking but I didnt ask Mum if she was going to marry Uncle Alan because if I said it it might come true.

In the evening the Pub got more busy than ever with people coming for the Karaoke.

I was sitting on a stool behind the bar because I wanted to be there to spy on Mum and Uncle Alan. But when Uncle Alan sang his first song I wished I wasnt there. He sang with his eyes squeezed shut like he was on the toilet and couldnt go and his face went red and he held his fist near his heart and he sang really LOUD. And when he finished he waited for everyone to clap like Emperor Nero when he sang rubbish songs on his lyre which is like a guitar but smaller.

I thought about Emperor Nero and the palace he made called the Golden House which is where he played on his lyre and which I read about in one of my library books. No one liked the Golden House because it was built after the fire in Rome on top of the burnt buildings and that is why people thought Emperor Nero started the fire. The Golden House was the biggest palace ever and it had a massive statue of Emperor Nero and it was not like the Golden House in Newark which is a Chinese. It was much bigger with lots of gold and pillars.

Uncle Alan sang Elvis songs. Elvis was fat like Uncle Alan and Emperor Nero but Elvis was a good singer. I have heard him on the jukebox. But Uncle Alan is a bad singer and he sang a song which was WE CANT GO ON TOGETHER WITH SUSPICIOUS MINDS and it was a good job he closed his eyes when he sang because everyone was making faces. Well Mum wasnt but everyone else was. But everyone clapped at the end because everyone is a bit scared of Uncle Alan I think apart from Big Vic who said Thank God for that.

Then after the song he said One more from the King.

Big Vic said Elvis leave the building.

But Uncle Alan ignored Big Vic and he sang another song which was WISE MEN SAY ONLY FOOLS RUSH IN BUT I CANT HELP FALLING IN LOVE WITH YOU. He had his eyes open and he was looking at Mum and it wasnt really singing it was speaking and Mum was smiling and crying at the same time and it made me feel heavy I dont know why like the ceiling was getting lower and squeezing all the air on top of me.

I stopped looking at Mum and Uncle Alan and I looked round the Pub at the people and they were all looking at Uncle Alan. Well everyone except Carla the Barmaid who was scratching her arm and looking at me. When she saw me looking back she shrugged up her shoulders and smiled and the smile tried to lift up the air but it didnt.

Uncle Alan finished talking the song and started talking his own words which were Right if Im allowed to borrow your ears for a few more moments Ive got something of a special announcement to make.

I looked at Mum and her face changed when he said announcement. Her eyes started normal at ANN but then they went bigger at OUNCE and then very wide at MENT and Uncle Alans eyes were looking at Mum but he didnt know her eyes meant STOP because he kept going like a car with no brakes.

Uncle Alan said As many of you know myself and Carol have grown a lot closer over the last two months as we have tried to come to terms with the TRAGIC loss of Brian.

And then he kept on talking and I wasnt listening because I hate his voice and dont like to let it in my ears but I heard the last bit which was Which is why us two fools have decided to rush in and tie the knot.

I looked round at the shocked faces and the slow rising

glasses and the lights going up and down on the machines and Mum looking at me. Behind Mum there was Carla the Barmaid with her thin lips open like an O like the shape of her earrings and Big Vic said in his loud voice Blimey and Les Miserable said in his quiet voice Bloody Hell. I had to get out and I left the stool and I went into the hall and then upstairs and I heard Mum follow. I went into the Living Room and I saw the PlayStation and I saw the poker and I picked up the poker with its gold handle like a sword and I picked it up and I pulled out the PlayStation on the carpet and I smashed it SMASH!

I made the PlayStation open up and I saw all the wires and the metal and I kept on smashing. SMASH! SMASH! SMASH!

And Mum was out of the bar and running up the stairs and she saw me and screamed PHILIP!

And there was another voice and it was Uncle Alan and he said What the?

And I turned round with the poker sword and Uncle Alan said Put it down son.

I said Im not your son.

He said Put it down!

Mum shouted Philip put it down!

And I said Wheres your ring? Wheres your ring?

Uncle Alan said Shes not wearing it because she didnt know how to tell you.

Mum said You didnt have to tell the whole Pub.

Uncle Alan said Why not? Weve got nothing to be ashamed of.

And I looked at Mums hands which were digging into the sofa she was standing behind.

That was when Uncle Alans hands grabbed me.

They were so strong I had no choice so I dropped the poker and he looked at me and said Now listen SON. What are you going to do about that?

I looked in his eyes and I wondered if Sleepy Eye Terry told him about what happened on Halloween. I wondered if that was why Uncle Alan told the Pub about getting married before telling me.

I said About what?

He said About the present I bought you.

And his voice was really quiet which was more scary than when it was really loud and his eyes were hating me and the hating was not mixed with anything else just hate and hate.

Mum was there and saying Alan please. Hes just upset. Hes just

Uncle Alan said Upset? Upset? Ill give him upset.

I said Let me go.

And I could see in his face he wanted to hit me. He was going red like the redness was the hit that was inside him that he wanted to give but he couldnt because Mum was there and Mum said Please.

That is all she said.

Dancing Queen

And Uncle Alans hands let go of me and I went to my room and I wanted to see Dads Ghost but he was nowhere.

I heard Mum and Uncle Alan row about Uncle Alan telling the Pub and the row was mixed with the singing from downstairs and the song was Abba. It was YOU ARE THE DANCING QUEEN which was Mums favourite. It was Carla the Barmaid singing and she sang very sad and I could hear Uncle Alans voice in the next room say Thats too far. Too far. Hes crossed the line this time.

And Mum said Hes been through a lot.

And Carla said Feel the beat from the tambourine.

And then Uncle Alan said more things. He said

He needs discipline.

He needs to be told he cant just go smashing things up.

Youre soft with him Carol.

Im sorry but you are.

And its no good for him.

No good for anyone.

He needs a strong hand.

And then Mum said something I couldnt hear and Uncle Alan said Its not natural Carol. Its not right. He needs

And I put my hands over my ears because his voice was like poison and I was humming YOU ARE THE DANCING QUEEN. I looked at Gertie in the tank swimming the other way to the Guppies and the black Mollies. When Gertie got to the end of the tank she turned and made herself invisible but I knew she was there and there was no light in the room only the tank but I didnt want to take my hands off my ears so I stayed in the dark. Outside the window there was Newark and the church and the steeple that pointed out from the flatness like a heart beat on a black screen that goes beep like on TV in hospitals and the church was yellow gold from the lights and it was pretty and sad and I dont know why but it was.

Then after a bit I took my hands off my ears. I heard Mum and Uncle Alan still talking.

Uncle Alan said We should move it forward.

Mum said What?

Uncle Alan said The Wedding.

Mum said The Wedding?

Uncle Alan said Listen.

Mum said What?

Uncle Alan said If youre right about Philip the last thing the poor lad wants is more uncertainty and instability in his life. If we get married Soon As then Job Done he knows where he stands and he can get on with his life.

Mum said I dont know.

Uncle Alan said You didnt know about the Pub either did you but that all turned out all right. The numbers speak for themselves. Weve got the bank off your back.

Mum said I know but

Uncle Alan said It makes sense. Trust me. A year from now we wont be seeing him smashing things up and getting into trouble. We just want to sort it out so we can you know move forward. Let me get on to the Registry Office.

His voice went different. It went slow and low and I heard kissing noises and then I heard Uncle Alan say If we get on to the Registry Office we could have it all done in a month. Its what we both want isnt it? Come on. Whats stopping us now?

The word went over and over in my brain Now now now now now.

Mum said I dont. Oh I dont. Alan. I dont know.

But then her words stopped being words and started being noises and I knew this meant they were kissing and Uncle Alan was eating her words with his big dry mouth and whisky and crisp breath.

And that is when I left my room and went quiet down the stairs with the carpet patterns changing under my feet and Big Vic was singing START SPREADING THE NEWS IM LEAVING TODAY and that is when I opened the back door.

The Ghost Wind

I walked out to the three Bottle Banks and I went to the right of them and I said I am Philip Noble. My Dad is Brian Noble. He is in your club.

Nothing happened so I said I want to speak to my dad. Do you know where my dad is?

Dads Ghost might have been having the Terrors but I thought he was angry with me for not killing Uncle Alan yet.

I said Ray Goodwin. Do you know where my dads ghost is?

I looked in the air and looked on the ground at the broken glass and there was a carrier bag that said Morrisons from the Supermarket and just after I asked the question it filled with air and floated up. It started flying out of the car park so I followed it because this was the Answer.

The bag went onto the road and then up the street past the Palace Theatre and past some shops and past the Golden House and it kept going. It went past the Traffic Lights and the hospital and there was nobody about just some cars swooshing and one man walking a black dog that was so black it looked like a walking hole. The bag went into a real hole in a hedge and so I pushed myself through the hedge and wrecked my clothes and kept going until it got to the graveyard with all the graves like people in beds with duvets made of grass. I knew that was what the Dead Fathers were trying to say that Dads Ghost was here because when the bag went past Dads grave it touched it before flying up over the houses on the other side. I looked at Dads grave in the half dark.

Brian Peter Noble
10 December 1963 – 25 September 2005
A Beloved Father and Husband
Rest In Peace

And I said a word under my breath and it wasnt Dad and it wasnt Dead. It was something in the middle. For one minute I thought it was impossible that Dad was dead. He was still so real in my head I could smell him and hear his voice but once everybody was as real as Dad even Emperor Nero or Julius Caesar or Alexander the Great and they will have sneezed and jumped in their sleep and now they are nothing. Then I looked next to Dads grave at the metal box for the flowers with the holes in the top like a radio. I could see it in the dark and I wondered why there were no flowers in there because Mum normally put flowers in there but there were no flowers in there and that is when I saw the white light come up through the holes in thin lines and the lines were blurry and joined together and became a shape like a man like Dad and it was Dads Ghost.

And Dads Ghost looked cross and said Philip What are you doing here?

I said Nothing. Coming to find you because I wanted to see you because because you were right. Theyre getting married. Im sorry. Im sorry.

He said You are too distracted Philip.

I said Why?

He said The girl Philip. Your girlfriend.

I said Leah.

He said Yes.

I looked through him to the other side of the graveyard and there were some boys shouting by a bench under the trees.

Dads Ghost said You must not see her any more. You must tell her you are not Going Out together.

I said Why?

He said If you are to protect her and protect yourself you must stay on your own. Just you.

I said Why?

He said You cannot risk thinking about anything else Philip. Trust me. We are running out of time.

I said OK.

And then he said You must tell her as soon as possible. You must have no friends and no girlfriends and no distractions until this is over Philip. Its for your own good. I will come with you.

I said What?

He said I will come with you to the girls house.

I said No.

But he was already leading the way.

We got close to the boys by the bench and I saw who it was and they saw me so I stopped still and Dads Ghost stopped still and said Philip? What are you doing?

I said Dad wait.

Dominic Weekly said Its the Skitso.

Jordan Harper was wearing a cap and he laughed and his fish eyes bulged and he said Look. Hes talking to himsen.

Dominic Weekly was riding dead slow on his mountain bike while all the other boys were walking by his side and he said He thinks he can talk to his dad. The radgey.

And Jordan said in a silly high voice Hes not got his girl-friend to protect him.

I tried to say something but I was scared and Dominic Weekly got off his mountain bike and put it by a grave and it was total dark now.

Dominic Weekly said If we kill you then you can speak to your dad all you want.

Another boy I didnt know said to Dominic Smack him.

I didnt see what happened I just fell on the floor.

My head was killing and it hurt so bad it was hurting out-side my head not just inside. Like the whole graveyard was part of my headache.

I tried to get up but a foot went into me and pushed all the air out of me. Another foot kicked my bum and my face went into the ground into the grass and I said Dad! Help me Dad!

And I saw white go past my eyes and it was Dads Ghost fly-ing and I tried to get up. I got halfway and there was laughing and then a few seconds later I heard Dads Ghost in the air say Ray! He needs help.

And it started. The wind. It started blowing really hard and Dominic pushed me on the ground again and punched me and the wind blew harder and louder and Dominics bike fell over. I looked up and Jordan was leaning forward in the wind and his cap blew off his head and flew over to the tree. He put his hands on his head and then ran after it and the wind stole the other boys caps and the Morrisons bag flew into Dominics face. He shouted but I couldnt hear what he said and then he got rid of the bag on his face and picked up his bike and rode off with the other boys chasing their caps.

I sat by a gravestone that was going mouldy like a slice of bread so the wind wasnt as strong and the pain was still beating in my head. When the wind stopped I walked back to the street and followed Dads Ghost to Leahs.

The Fish in the Sea

Dads Ghost said Knock on the door.

I knocked on the door and it was Mr Fairview and his old long face looked at my suit all messy from the hedge and he said What in the name of God?

And I said Is Leah there please?

Mr Fairview looked at his watch but Leah must have heard me because she was there behind him and she said Dad.

She made a face which told Mr Fairview to go away and Mr Fairview went away because he is not like normal parents who are strict with their own children and nice to others. Mr Fairview thinks Leah is an Angel but I think he thinks Dane is the Devil because Mr Fairview went back in the house and rowed with Dane.

Leah coughed and said I think Im getting ill.

She stepped outside her door which was the back door because she doesnt use the front door and she went into the back garden where Dads Ghost and me were standing. She looked at my clothes and the bits of hedge on them and said You look like youve grown out of the garden.

And Dads Ghost said Tell her now.

I took her wrist and held her hard and Dads Ghost was behind saying Now Philip. You must tell her now.

I looked in Leahs eyes and they were scared of me and I didnt want her to be scared of me and she said Why you acting mental?

I was holding onto her arm too tight because she said Youre hurting me. Get off.

Her words went slow into my brain and I didnt get off in time so she pulled her arm away and she said Say something.

Dads Ghost said Tell her.

My mouth opened like a Guppy but no words came out.

Dane shouted inside the house Get off me you old cunt!

I kept trying to speak but all the words were too far away like the yellow ducks in the Goose Fair in Nottingham that I tried to get with the long stick and could never get even when I could see them in front of me.

Dad said Tell her Philip. Tell her you cant see her any more.

But her eyes were still the eyes behind the wheelie bins yesterday that could steal anything even my words and I looked at Dads Ghost and she looked behind her to see who I was looking at. She thought I was looking at her dad not my dads ghost because Mr Fairview had stopped rowing with Dane and was watching out of the window and she turned and said Dad!

She flicked her hands for Mr Fairview to go away and as she flicked her hands her fingers went inside Dads Ghost but she didnt notice. Then she looked back at me and my head was waving up and down and I still didnt have any words so I sighed and this made her frown. Then I closed my eyes and walked to the gate with my eyes still closed because I didnt want to see

Leahs eyes or Dads Ghosts eyes and I hit the gate so I opened it and ran off and left Leah just standing there and Dads Ghost running with me all the way home.

When I got there Uncle Alan was drunk in the hallway with everyone in the Pub behind. He said You look like youve been dragged through a hedge backwards.

Mum came and said Oh Philip where have you been.

I said Theres no flowers.

Mum said What?

I said Theres no flowers by Dads grave.

Mum said Is that where youve been?

I said Yes.

Mum said Oh Philip.

I looked at Uncle Alan and tried to set fire to him with my eyes while Mum came to me.

Uncle Alan didnt like Mum hugging me and picking bits of hedge off me I think he was jealous and so he said Mr Fairview has been on the blower. He says youve been there as well. Reckons youre mad about little Leah and thats why youre acting a bit strange. Has Leah dumped you Philip? Is that whats the matter? Plenty more fish in the sea son. Every dog has his day. Just look at me. Found the woman of my dreams at this time in life.

Uncle Alan winked at me and it was a nasty wink and now he was getting married to Mum he was not going to even pretend to like me.

And Uncle Alan said Mr Fairview is my Business Partner Philip. So I dont want you going and upsetting him. You hear me?

Mum stopped hugging me and said with a smile all flickery like a flame that is outside Come on Alan. Its been a long day.

And he looked at a bin liner in the hall with the PlayStation in it. He was going to say something else but he didnt. He just breathed out of his whistling nose and he sipped his whisky but he kept on looking at me and I was getting more scared and more scared and I went upstairs and into my room and stared at my fish until my heart went normal.

Mr Wormwood and the
Melting Point of Metals

I woke up in the morning and didnt see Dads Ghost because he was having the Terrors but I didnt need Dads Ghost because I knew what I had to do. I had to finish Leah and kill Uncle Alan. But at breakfast I pretended to be all right about Mum and Uncle Alan getting married and I said Im sorry.

Mum said What?

I said Im sorry. Im sorry about the PlayStation.

Mum said Well dont tell me. Tell Alan.

Mum wasnt calling him Uncle Alan now because she was getting married to him. It was just Alan and she didnt tell me she was getting rid of the Uncle bit she just did.

I said Im sorry Uncle Alan. Im sorry I smashed up the PlayStation.

He looked at me and then he looked at Mum washing up and he looked at Mums bum and he said Its all right Philip. Im sure it wont happen again.

I knew Uncle Alan was only pretending it was all right because his eyes said he wanted to throw me out of the window into the car park but I ignored his eyes and kept eating the Frosties going soft in the going sweet milk.

Mum looked at the ROTA which was on the wall and Mum said Carlas on tonight with Nooks.

Nooks is what Mum calls Renuka and ever since Dad died she helped behind the bar one night in the week making big heads on the beer.

And Mum said I reckon Carla could manage to be without us tonight. Why dont we get a video out and have a nice night in. Just the three of us.

The idea went KABOOM in Uncle Alans head because he was still mad about the PlayStation and maybe Sleepy Eye Terry as well. His lips and skin shook a bit because of the explosion but he said Why not?

And Mum turned round with her Make Up and Fake Up on and said Philip?

And I said Ill get a video on the way back from school.

Mum smiled and the smile hurt the love part of my brain and made it heavy. But I smiled back and still pretended.

Uncle Alan looked at me with his hot burning eyes like he hated the air I filled like he wanted it to be just empty space like how he made Dad just empty space like he wanted it just him and Mum.

I was going to dump Leah at break but she was off sick and Dane said she had a cough and I didnt think he knew Id been round last night and heard him row with his dad.

Dominic and Jordan walked past me and laughed and then they saw I was with Dane so they didnt pick on me. But I had to

see them again in Science lesson with Mr Wormwood and they
sat on the back row and Dominic said Oi Skitso. Spoke to your
dad lately?

They started telling everyone about seeing me in the graveyard but they stopped when Mr Wormwood came in.

Everyone is scared of Mr Wormwood even Dane probably
because Mr Wormwood is two metres tall and very skinny. He
speaks very quiet but will suddenly SHOUT REALLY LOUD
and make you jump. He has put black tape on the glass in his
Science Lab door and the tape is in bars like a prison and he has
a sign on the door that says **DO NOT FEED THE ANIMALS**.
He thinks it is funny but its not because children are animals
and so are grown ups so he is not a zookeeper he is just an older
animal. Children dont change into different animals when they
grow up. It is not like they are caterpillars going into butterflies.
They just get taller and wider and less funny and do jobs and
tell more lies like Uncle Alan.

Science is my worst subject because I dont believe in it because Science doesnt believe in ghosts and I know ghosts are
real. Science says that people know more and more about everything which is a lie and that everything can be explained and
that is another lie. There was a man called Sir Isaac Newton who
invented Science who said that apples fall down off trees because of Gravity and everyone thinks that is really clever. But
everyone knew apples fell off trees before its just they didnt
know it was because of Gravity. So it doesnt matter if its because
of Gravity or if its because of God or if its a big magnet under
the ground because apples still fall off trees. You can still eat
them whatever and they still taste the same which is gross especially when theyve got bruises on them that are brown and
mushy powder in your mouth from falling on the ground.

In Mr Wormwoods class we dont do things with apples. We just do things with Bunsen Burners and Test Tubes and Goggles and burn liquids till they change colour.

But I was pleased Mr Wormwood came in because then everyone stopped laughing at me.

Mr Wormwood tapped his ruler and said Settle down. Settle down.

Everyone was squeaking their stools on the floor and Mr Wormwood said in his calm voice Today God help me we are going to be testing the properties of different metals.

He looked round the room at all his animals and he squinted like we hurt his eyes.

He said Now does everyone understand what I mean by properties?

Dominic Weekly called out Houses.

Jordan laughed.

Mr Wormwood said in a voice getting louder OUT OUT OUT GET OUT GET OUT BOTH OF YOU GET OUT!

Dominic said But

Jordan said But

Mr Wormwood said OUT! He pointed at the door and Dominic and Jordan went out of the door and Mr Wormwood went out of the door and shut the door and shouted at them for two minutes. Then Dominic and Jordan came back in the class all pale and Mr Wormwood came in to the front of the class combing his hair with his hand.

He said in his calm voice Properties are characteristics that describe something. That set it apart from other types of substance.

Mr Wormwood got some chalk and went to the blackboard and read in his head from a sheet and wrote

THE PROPERTIES OF METALS:
Strength (except tin)
Can conduct heat and electricity
Ductility (ability of metal to be drawn into a wire)
Shiny
Sonorous

Mr Wormwood pointed to Sonorous and said Can anyone tell me what this word means?

Charlotte Ward put up her hand.

Mr Wormwood said Charlotte.

Charlotte said Is it to do with the way it sounds?

Mr Wormwood said The way it sounds. Yes. The way it sounds. If you drop a metal it will make a sound and what sort of sound would it make Charlotte? What sort of sound?

Charlotte said A clanking sound?

Mr Wormwood said Good good. A clanking sound. Thank you Charlotte. If you drop metal on the floor it clanks while if you dropped Dominic or Jordan on the floor it would be more of a thud.

Mr Wormwood smiled because he had made a joke but no one laughed because everyone was scared.

Mr Wormwood said Can anyone think of any other properties metal might have? Anyone? Anyone? Yes Charlotte.

Charlotte said Theyre magnetic.

Mr Wormwood sucked in her words through his nose as if they had a smell and it was a smell he didnt know if he liked or not. He said Mmmmm most metals are not magnetic actually. Only some metals. Like iron.

He wrote another word on the blackboard.

The word was

Malleability

Mr Wormwood pointed to it with the chalk and said Anyone? Anyone?

But no one not even Charlotte knew what Malleability was.

Mr Wormwood said in a super fast super quiet voice If something is Malleable it can be made to change its shape and keep its mass by using a degree of heat or force and this makes it different from other solid materials like wood or stone or Year Seven pupils.

This was another joke but no one laughed because they were still scared.

Mr Wormwood said On the benches in front of you you will see a glass jar with a type of metal contained inside it.

There was a jar between me and the person next to me who was Siraj. The jar had a label on it and it said **COPPER** and there was a shiny orange square of metal inside it.

Mr Wormwood said One of the properties that changes from metal to metal is the melting point. So we are going to test different metals over a flame.

We had to get into Partners and Siraj looked round quick for someone else to be Partner with but everyone was with someone so he had to be with me.

I said Its Copper.

He said What?

I said Weve got Copper.

He said Really?

I said Yes.

He said Duh.

And then we got all the equipment out and I pushed the Bunsen Burners rubber tube onto the tap that let out the methane.

Siraj used to like me but he doesnt like me now. If Jordan and Dominic dont like you then no one dares like you. They all just act like Jordan and Dominic but not so strong like Jordan and Dominic are orange squash but the other boys are like orange squash with water in. All the boys are now Jordan and Dominic flavour just a bit milder but still with a bad taste so not like orange squash like methane squash.

I thought I didnt want to finish Leah because when she was at school everyone left me alone but when she wasnt there like at the graveyard they all got at me. But then I thought of Dads Ghost and I said in my head I will finish her.

We put on our Goggles and then we did the Experiment with me picking up the piece of Copper in tongs and Siraj holding the Bunsen Burner and leaning it so none of the metal went in.

Mr Wormwood told us to try melting it on the yellow flame first which is 400 degrees Centigrade and I held it with the tongs right in the flame.

I said Its not melting.

Siraj made big eyes in his goggles and said Really?

I said No.

Charlotte Ward and Sarah Keane were on the bench in front and their metal was melting and making silver bubbles on the Heat Proof Mat.

Then Siraj turned the Bunsen Burner to the blue flame which was 600 degrees and the Copper stayed hard because it wasnt at its melting point. And I said Its still not melting.

Siraj said Really?

And then it was the end of the Experiment and if the metal melted on the yellow flame it had a low melting point and if it melted on the blue flame it had a medium melting point and if it didnt melt at all it had a high melting point and then we all had to tell which one ours was and Mr Wormwood wrote it on the board.

LOW MELTING POINT
Tin
Zinc
Lead
MEDIUM MELTING POINT
Aluminium
HIGH MELTING POINT
Iron

I saw something flicker outside the window with the **DO NOT FEED THE ANIMALS** sign.

Mr Wormwood said something and I wasnt listening and he said Earth calling Philip Noble. Earth to Philip Noble. Is anyone there? Come in Philip Noble do you receive me?

And this was another joke but everyone laughed this time.

I said Yes Sir.

He said Did the Copper melt?

The question was like a jigsaw I had to put together in my brain.

Then Mr Wormwood said Did. The. Copper. Melt? In your own time.

I said No Sir.

He said in a silly voice No Sir.

Everyone laughed again and then he wrote Copper on the board under Iron.

I said to Siraj I didnt hear him.

Siraj said Really?

I said No.

Mr Wormwood turned round and reached his melting point and said SHUT UP SHUT UP SHUT UP BOY!

And when Mr Wormwood turned round again Siraj made a

spacca face at me and Jordan or Dominic threw a pencil at my head. The pencil landed on the floor and Mr Wormwood turned round and said Philip Noble if you are not interested in what I have to say perhaps you might like to take the rest of the lesson?

I said No Sir.

He said in his silly voice No Sir.

Everyone laughed again.

Mr Wormwood said Well in that case why dont you put everyones equipment away for them?

So I had to put all the equipment away and I looked out of the door window and I could see Dads Ghost looking at me and everyone else was crowding round the Front Bench to watch Mr Wormwood do an Experiment.

I put all the Bunsen Burners in the cupboard and then I got the bits of melted metal on the Heat Proof Mats and I went to the sink and poured them in.

Mr Wormwood said NOT THE SINK! NOT THE SINK YOU DOZY SPECIMEN! PUT THE BITS IN THE BIN! NOT THE SINK! SWEET MOTHER OF MOSES!

When I was putting all the bits in the bin and putting all the tongs in the drawer and all the Heat Proof Mats in the cupboard Mr Wormwood showed the class what happened to another metal under a flame. He wrote the metal on the board and it was Magnesium.

And when I was in one of the cupboards I heard the whole class breathe in fast. I looked round and there was a massive bright white flame and funny smoke like candyfloss and a fizzy sound.

I saw Dads Ghost still in the window and he was moving his hand for me to come. I looked at Mr Wormwood and all the class and they were looking at the flame and so I put my hand up and said Sir can I go to the toilet?

Mr Wormwood said Cant it wait?

I said Im dying.

Mr Wormwood said Jesus boy. All right. Be quick.

I went to the door and opened it and closed it and Dad pointed to the store cupboard next to the classroom and he said Its open.

I said What?

He said Open it.

I said What?

He said Open it.

I said But

He said He forgot to lock it.

I looked through the window to see if anyone could see me but they were all looking at the flame.

Dads Ghost said This is your chance.

I said Chance?

He said To get what you need to kill Uncle Alan.

I said But

He said Youre not weakening on me?

I thought of him saving me from Dominic and Jordan yesterday and I said No.

He said Well then. Open the door. Ill keep an eye on your Teacher.

I opened the door and felt scared like when I got in the mini bus.

There were shelves and shelves and shelves and boxes and bottles and Dads Ghost looked inside and pointed to a small bottle of something that looked like water and he said Take that.

I looked at the label and it said

ETHANOL

WARNING: Poisonous/Flammable

I put the bottle in my pocket and I saw another small bottle full of something that looked like sugar and it said

METALLIC SODIUM

WARNING: Will explode on contact with water

I put that in my other pocket and Dads Ghost said Quick quick. Hes nearly finished the Experiment.

I saw a box that said **MAGNESIUM GRANULES** and it was too big to put in my pocket so I kept it in my hand and Dads Ghost said Quick quick quick!

I got out of the store cupboard and closed the door and I couldnt go back in the class and get my bag because Mr Wormwood would see me with the box so I just ran down the corridor and kept on going until I was at the toilets. I hid until the bell went and no one came to check on me I dont know why.

Dads Ghost came and said to me Your bags still in the classroom.

I went out of the toilets and the corridor was quiet because everyone was at break. When I got to the classroom I went in and got my bag and put all the stuff in it and then I went out of the lab and checked the Science stock room but it was locked.

Ray Ray Goodwin

Later on I had another meeting with Mrs Fell and she was wearing a pink clip in her curly hair and a T shirt that was tight and she was smiling at me with her mouth but not with her eyes which were tired. I put my bag down gently so I didnt leak the poison or start the exploding powder.

Then when I sat down I told her Mums marrying Uncle Alan.

Her face kept smiling but her pupils changed and the black circles got bigger and nearly squeezed out all the green.

She said Oh.

I dont think she could think of what to say and then she said I see. Right.

And then she said And what do you FEEL about that Philip?

I said I dont know.

She said Do you like your uncle?

I gave a No with my head.

She said But surely you like to see your mother happy?

I lifted my shoulders one at a time and then I said I want to stop it.

She said You want to stop them getting married?

I said Yes.

I looked on her shelf and there was a picture of a man. It looked a bit like the man in the wheelchair I saw in the park but this man wasnt in a wheelchair.

Mrs Fell said If your mum wants to marry someone you have to let her Philip.

And then she said Why did you not go back to Mr Wormwoods Science lesson earlier today? He said that you took a very long time in the toilet.

Mrs Fell had a look in her face like she wanted to save me from something but the look made me want to save her from something and then she would see me not just as a boy and then she would ask me different questions.

She said My dad died you know Philip? Can you remember I told you?

I shook my head because I couldnt remember.

She said I still picture him walking out the door on the last day I saw him.

I said What was your dad?

She said He was a miner. A coal miner. He used to have to go deep underground and work in the dark.

She didnt say anything for a bit and then she told me about the Strikes when people didnt go to work because they didnt want the mines to close.

I said Was your dad on strike?

And she said Yes at first but my mum was very ill. My dad

wanted to still work and earn money for better treatment for her. And people were cross with him in Ollerton which is where Im from because he broke the Strike.

I thought of the man in the wheelchair in the park near the castle and I thought of something else and I said What was your dads name?

And she said Ray Ray Goodwin.

It felt weird and my hands were wet and I didnt know what to say and the room went small round me.

Ray Ray Goodwin.

Ray Ray Goodwin.

And I knew it wasnt really Ray Ray Goodwin it was just Ray Goodwin. It was Ray Goodwin who was in the Dead Fathers Club but I had to check when he died.

She said 11 years ago.

I was going to tell her that Ray Goodwin tried to speak to her and I was going to tell her everything. But then I thought that Ray Goodwin was out of the No Time because he had passed more than one birthday and so he was for ever in the Terrors. So even if she believed in Ray Goodwins ghost it was too late to help him escape the Terrors and get Revenge.

She said Philip? Philip? Are you all right? Philip?

I said Yes.

And I thought if I told her she wouldnt believe me or she would feel sad for her dads ghost and I didnt want her to feel sad or to hate me so I stayed quiet.

She didnt say he died of murder but I knew she was thinking it because she closed her eyes and did a big breath and a swallow. And I thought I bet it was one of the miners who hated him but I didnt want to ask Mrs Fell because she might cry.

She said Its very hard when someone you love dies Philip.

You feel like a bit of you has died as well. But you do get over it Philip. Eventually.

The bell went and Mrs Fell just looked at me with sad shoulders. I wanted her to hug me and to put my head in her warm boobs for ever. But that wasnt going to happen so I picked up my bag with my weapons in it and I went out.

The Changemaker

In the toilet at break I said to Dads Ghost about Mrs Fells Dad being Ray Goodwin and he said What did you tell her about the club?

I said Nothing.

He said Good. Good. Even if you told her she wouldnt believe you. Ray always talks about her but he gets upset because she cant see him.

I said Why can I see you and Mrs Fell cant see her dad?

I heard two boys come into the toilets so I made sure the door was locked and my hand went through Dads Ghost.

I said Sorry.

He said Its OK.

He said There are different types of ghosts. There are ghosts people can see and ghosts people cant see. And the ghosts people cant see try to learn special powers so they can influence the living.

I said What powers?

He said Rays a Changemaker.

I said Whats a Changemaker?

He said Some ghosts can change things among the living like change the wind.

I thought about the Morrisons carrier bag and the wind that blew Dominic and Jordan away.

I wondered if Uncle Alan could be blown away by the wind and I said Will you ever be able to do things like that?

Dads Ghost said Ray says all ghosts have the potential but I dont know. Ray gives classes at the club. I find it hard.

I said Oh.

He said Dont tell Mrs Fell anything Philip. You mustnt tell anyone anything. You do understand?

I said Yes.

And then I heard laughing outside the door because I was talking to myself and Dads Ghost faded into the Terrors and I kept the toilet door locked until the laughing boys disappeared.

I saw my bag on the ground and it was in a little puddle and I didnt want the things I took from the store cupboard to get wet because then they might explode. I put the bag on my back and lifted the seat and tried to have a wee but nothing came out.

The Murder of Gonzago

I had the poison and the granules and the explosives in my bag
but before I killed Uncle Alan I had to definitely know for
DEFINITE that it was him who did Dads brakes.

So I went to Players the video shop like Mum said and there
were lots of DVDs to choose from. Lots were 18s and 15s and I
couldnt get them out even though they looked better than the
12s and PGs and the Us but I wasnt looking for a good film because I didnt care about films any more. I was looking for a film
that I knew Uncle Alan wouldnt like and so I looked at the
backs to see the stories.

I was there for ages reading all the backs and then I got to a
film called The Murder of Gonzago and it said on the cover

A BROTHER's MURDER. A SON's REVENGE

SET IN ITALY IN THE BLOOD-SOAKED DAYS BEFORE THE
ROMAN REPUBLIC, *THE MURDER OF GONZAGO* TELLS THE

THRILLING STORY OF DUKE FORTIMUS (JOAQUIN PHOENIX), WHO MURDERS HIS BROTHER, GONZAGO THE KING (ACADEMY AWARD WINNER MEL GIBSON), IN ORDER TO MARRY QUEEN LIVIA (ACADEMY AWARD WINNER CHARLIZE THERON), AND TAKE THE THRONE. IT IS THEN LEFT TO THE MURDERED KING'S ONLY SON, HONORARIUS, (TOBEY MAGUIRE—*SPIDERMAN*, *SEABISCUIT*) TO TAKE HIS VIOLENT REVENGE.

'MY REVENGE WILL COME . . .'

And my hands started to shake because I thought this was how I could tell for DEFINITE that it was Uncle Alan who killed Dad because I would watch his face because he can never hide the signs on his face. I looked to see what it was and it was a 12 and I went to the counter and the man with boobs who was watching the small TV behind the counter beeped my card and said Back tomorrow by seven and I said OK and went home.

When I got to the Pub I went and put my weapons in a Hiding Place under my bed and then went into the kitchen. Renuka was there having a cup of coffee with Mum and she said Hello Philip.

I said Hello.

She said Ah like it was my first word and she looked at the DVD and said Is that a DVD?

I thought No its a jam sandwich but I didnt say that because I like Renuka really its just she thinks all children are two year olds so I said Yes. Its the Murder of Gonzago.

She said Right.

I said Its about a man who kills his brother.

Renuka said Right.

Mum looked at me funny as she blew her coffee and Renuka said to Mum Is that the one with Russell Crowe?

And Mum said I dont know.

Renuka said I love Russell Crowe. Him and whatshisface. The Irish one. With the nice bum.

Mum said Colin Farrell.

Renuka blew but not into her coffee just into the air and said Imagine both of them.

Then she laughed and said Sorry Philip cover your ears.

Renuka has a funny face. It is like an upside down triangle with big round eyes and a stick body and perfect skin like she is made by computers not by a mum and a dad. After her coffee she went downstairs and left her smell which is soap.

I said Wheres Uncle Alan?

Mum said Why?

I said I want to watch the film.

Mum said Hes still at the Garage. Hes got a lot of work on. Well watch the film later.

I said When are you getting married?

Mum looked into her cup and then she stood up and looked everywhere but not in my eyes and said I dont know Philip. We dont know yet.

I said Will it be before Dads Birthday?

The question hit her on the nose.

She said Philip please.

I said December the 10th.

She said in a cross voice I know perfectly well when Dads Birthday is. Was. Is.

Mums cross voice was catching and I said Do you know when his deathday is?

She said Philip

I said Do you know when it was? When he died? How many days? How many days?

Mum picked up the tea towel but there was nothing to dry.

I said Uncle Alan said two months but its less. Dads body wont be a skeleton yet. And he wont be a skeleton when you have the Wedding.

The second time I said skeleton Mum started crying into the tea towel and then I felt bad so I said Im sorry and I kept saying it until there were enough Im sorrys for her to stop.

It took nine.

Later we watched the film with Uncle Alan sitting in Dads chair with his glass of gold whisky in his dirty hands. He was just changed out of his blue uniform into his popper shirt and Mum had her legs up on the sofa drinking her DIET Lemonade and I got the controls and I pressed play.

The film started and there were lots of bits I didnt understand and then there was a bit with the Queen finding out the King is dead and the Queen said The only woman who would marry a second time is one who would kill her first husband.

I looked at Mum and she was still upset about me saying about Dads skeleton and so she didnt like the Queen saying that. It was like the words had a taste and she had to drink a bit of lemonade.

Then the film went back in time to when the King was living and his brother says I will trap my brother like a mouse.

I looked at Uncle Alans face and the shadows on his face changed like he was biting his teeth really hard and then it went to the best bit.

This was the bit when the King was sleeping on his own. His brother went in and poured poison in his ear like how Dad poured medicine into my ear to get rid of wax. I looked at Uncle Alan and his face went redder than normal and the shadows on his face started to shake like he was a volcano like in Pompeii about to burst with lava coming out of the top of his head but he wasnt a volcano so he just stood up and said Its too dark in here.

But it wasnt very dark because the little light was on near the TV but Uncle Alan said Lets have some light.

He switched the main lights on and then he sat down. But it was like the film was making his chair get really hot because he kept on standing up and doing things like pouring some more whisky. Then he looked out of the curtains at the car park and at the Bottle Banks and the Dead Fathers Club that he couldnt see and he said Its getting pretty busy I might go downstairs and give Carla a hand behind the bar.

He looked at the screen and it was the bit when the Queen married again even though she said she wouldnt.

Mum said Oh dont you want to watch the rest of the film?

He said Its not really my thing. You know. These costume ones. I like modern ones really. Or the old cowboy stuff.

Mum said Oh OK.

Then Uncle Alan went downstairs.

So he did it!! He fixed Dads car for DEFINITE! Dads Ghost isnt lying! He did it! His volcano face was proof. Definite total proof!!

In the last bit of the film the Kings son who was Spiderman killed all the new Kings soldiers and chopped off their heads.

Mum said Oh Philip its a bit violent. Are you sure its only a 12?

I said Yes.

Spiderman had a big fight with his uncle and didnt wait because he wasnt a wimp and he said Prepare to die.

They had their swords out and inside my head I was saying Go on kill him! Kill your uncle!

And he did. He killed his uncle and all the Kings men which were there to trap him. And in the end it was just him and his mum and she was not cross with him because she knew the King was bad.

And at the names at the end Dads Ghost flickered on behind the TV and he didnt say anything he just watched me and Mum and the words Mum said to try and make me like Uncle Alan.

Uncle Alan loved Dad. He loved him Philip.

I know you want it just to be me and you Philip. I know you do. But one day you will be all grown up and leave home and I will be on my own all old and wrinkly and no one will want me Philip. You wouldnt want that would you?

Uncle Alan isnt going to replace Dad. No ones going to replace him.

If Im going to look after you Im going to need someone to look after me.

Hes a kind man. A very kind man. He might not be Brad Pitt but he cares about us Philip.

He wants to help Philip. Look what hes done for us with the Pub. He doesnt have to do all that does he? Does he? Does he? No he doesnt.

And Dads Ghost said Dont listen son. Dont listen.

So I didnt.

Slaves

The next morning I checked the poison and the explosives and the Magnesium were under the bed in their Hiding Place and then I had breakfast early and I went to school early.

Mrs Palefort the Head Teacher did an assembly about Freedom and Slavery and started talking about trainers and about Brand Names like Pepsi and Nike and Adidas and McDonalds and PlayStation and Reebok and KFC and Billabong and Walkers and she said The word branding came from when farmers used to burn marks into their cows to show they belonged to them.

She made her eyes look like iced buns inside her thick glasses and she said When you wear your Nike trainers to school you might think you are expressing your freedom but really you are showing the world that you are owned by that PARTICULAR company.

I thought about the Roman bakers who marked their bread and I thought about the Roman Slave owners who marked their

Slaves when they tried to run away. And I thought that even if you never ever wore trainers or never ever turned into a cow or a loaf of bread you are not free because there is always something that is controlling you. There is the Cold Weather that says Put on a hat or the Teachers that say Go to assembly or the Police that say Dont steal from Boots or your Bladder that says Go to the toilet or Dads Ghost that says Kill Uncle Alan. You are never free because you are in your body and your body is a prison because you end up old and in pain like Nan and then you die. And your brain is a prison as well because you cannot switch off your thoughts and when you sleep you have bad dreams. And if you die it might still be like a prison because Dad is a ghost and he wants to escape being a ghost and just to be Nothing like before he was born. But he doesnt know if you can be Nothing again or if he will still be Something. No one knows for definite. Not even the Scientists like Mr Wormwood or the Religious People like Mr Fairview.

At break I went and sat on a bench in the yard on my own because Leah was still off with a cough. And Dominic threw his SAS bag at me and said Need your bodyguard?

He meant Leah.

I said No but I felt Yes inside.

The Colours in the Fish Tank

I went into my room after school. I went into it and it was different. It was warmer. There was a smell like tyres when they skid and I thought thats a weird smell but I didnt do anything. I just lay on my bed thinking if I was ever going to do anything about Uncle Alan or if I was just a wimp who does things in his head and not in real life. And that is when I saw it. That is when I saw the fish tank.

I looked at it when I was on the bed and I didnt know what was weird about it. Then I noticed the colours and the colours were green and black and blue and red and they were water clouds like what you make in Art when you put the paintbrush in the water. I thought Whos put paint in the fish tank?

And I got off the bed and went closer to the fish tank and I thought Where are the fish? Where is Gertie?

And I opened the lid which was warmer than normal and I looked with my head over the water and it was hot like when you have a bath and forget to put the cold in and it makes your feet red. But it was even hotter than that and it burnt my eyes.

The smell was strong like it was nearly a taste and it made me feel sick and I looked through the top of the water and it was hard to see because of the heat and the steam and the ripples but I made my eyes look. And I saw all the colours mixing together.

I looked for Gertie and I said Gertie which is stupid because fish dont speak human they speak fish. Then I saw something like a green bit of paper in the water and it was getting smaller and I felt very sick then and I looked at the heater and the heater said 120 not 82 and I dropped the lid and I thought of the Mollies melting and the five Guppies melting and Gertie still melting all her bones and her skin melting.

Dads Ghost came in the room and he said It was Uncle Alan. He turned up the heater.

I shouted No!

And I said in my head Hes dead hes dead hes dead Uncle Alan hes dead.

Mum came in and screamed and then Uncle Alan came in and it stayed in my head Hes dead hes dead hes dead.

Mums hand with shiny nails was over her mouth and she looked at the fish tank and then Uncle Alan looked and he pretended to be surprised but he wasnt a good pretender.

Dads Ghost was in the room and he was saying Dont act mad Philip. Thats what he wants. Thats why he did it. He wants you to go mad so no one will believe you about anything.

So I didnt act mad. I just said The heater was on 120 and not 82.

And I looked at Uncle Alan and he said It must have broke Philip.

He stared at me like he was trying to do a Mind Trick and Mum said behind her hand Oh oh oh.

Uncle Alan said Dont think well be having fish and chips tonight.

And he laughed HE LAUGHED and Dads Ghost looked at me and said Stay calm Philip. Stay calm.

Mum said Oh the smell.

And I stayed calm and watched Uncle Alan sort the tank with a jug and a bucket Mum got from downstairs and when most of the melted fish water was out he tried to pick up the tank but it was heavy with stones in the bottom and he said My back! My back!

I looked at the five Guppies all turned to water but I stayed calm.

Uncle Alan said Ill have to sort the rest out later Carol. Ive got to get the questions done.

He said it like a Pub Quiz was more important than my dead fish.

Dads Ghost said Tonight Philip. You can do it tonight.

I said Yes. Im going to.

And Uncle Alan and Mum looked at me like I was mad and then looked at Dads Ghost like he was just air and just nothing because they couldnt see him.

Dads Ghost said Good boy Philip. Good boy.

The Pub Quiz

The Pub was very busy for the first Pub Quiz night. I thought if Uncle Alan died tonight it might be anyone who killed him. So I got the little bottle of ETHANOL and I had it in my pocket. I went to Mum in her bedroom and said Can I watch the Pub Quiz tonight?

She was brushing her eyelashes in the mirror and she said Theres not much to watch. I thought youd want an Early Night. After what happened to your tank.

I tried not to think of Gertie and I said But can I?

She said Of course you can.

She waited a bit and then said We will get you some new fish Philip. If you want.

I didnt say anything. I didnt want a new dad and I didnt want new fish. Especially if Uncle Alan was paying for them.

I stayed sitting on her bed watching her in the mirror and I said If Dad came back tonight would you dump Uncle Alan?

She stopped brushing her eye hairs and looked at me not in the mirror in real life and she said What?

I said If Dad came back tonight would you dump Uncle Alan?

She said What kind of a question is that?

I lifted up my shoulders.

It wasnt like questions in a PUB QUIZ so I think it was a PRIVATE question not a PUBLIC question.

She sat next to me and said Philip sweetheart. Dad isnt going to come back.

I said But what if he did?

My words were making water in her eyes but she stopped the water falling because she didnt want to mess up her Make Up.

She said No one will ever replace your dad Philip. No one. Now come on.

She slapped my leg three times really quick which means in slap language Now come on.

I said I know.

She then did her hair with her hands and said How do I look?

I said Nice.

She said Were going up to see Nan at the weekend.

I said Oh.

I bet Mum hadnt told Nan yet about marrying Uncle Alan. I bet that was why we were going.

Mum got up and sprayed some perfume on her and I tasted it in my mouth and I saw her bra through her tight white top.

She said Are you coming down then?

I said Yes.

We went downstairs and sat on the table nearest to the MICROPHONE. All the other tables were set out with the teams and most of the people were talking so I couldnt hear anything just bubble bubble bubble.

Carla came over with her hoop earrings and her hoop eyes and her short skirt. She looked like two people sewn together. A young person on the bottom half and an old flaky person on the top half. Mum looked at Carlas legs like she was scared of them.

Carla gave Mum a glass of White Wine and gave me a glass of Pepsi and said A glass of White Wine and a glass of Pepsi.

Mum said Thanks Carla. Have you seen Alan anywhere?

Carla scratched her neck and said I think he was going to print out the things off the machine.

Mum said Right.

They looked at each other and smiled and something happened in the air in between the smiles and then Carla went back to the bar.

Uncle Alan came in holding some bits of paper and he held up the pieces of paper and some people clapped and someone did a whistle and Uncle Alan handed the Answer Sheets round and got to the microphone and switched it on. The microphone went nnnnnnn really loud and everyone put their fingers in their ears and he tried to stop the nnnnnnn but it kept going for ages and he said Bloody Dixons.

Everyone laughed and the nnnnnnn stopped and he tapped the microphone three times df df df.

He said Right. Lets get this show on the road.

I felt the bottle of poison in my pocket and watched as Carla went over and gave Uncle Alan his glass of whisky. Someone whistled again. It was a different kind of whistle. It was a Wolf Whistle and it was for Carlas young half not her old half.

Uncle Alan said Thanks Carla.

He looked at her legs and wanted to say something else but

he didnt because Mum was there behind him burning holes in his bad back with invisible laser beams out of her eyes.

He said Right. The first round is a general knowledge round. So if youve got your pens ready.

There was an Answer Sheet and pen on our table but Mum was only doing it for fun not for the £100. And I was only doing it to kill Uncle Alan and get REVENGE for Dad and Gertie and the Mollies and the five Guppies.

Uncle Alan said If you were born on June the 21st what would be your Star Sign?

Mum said Oh I know this one.

She wrote down GEMINI next to the one on the sheet.

Uncle Alan put his whisky down on our table and he winked at Mum and breathed loud breath into the microphone. And then he said OK question two. Bit of a tricky one this. Who was the second wife of Henry the 8th?

Mum looked at me and said Have you done this one at school Philip?

I said No.

Mum said I think Ill just take a guess.

She wrote JOAN OF ARK on the paper.

I looked at the glass of whisky and all the lights in it shining from the fruit machines and the ceiling and I looked at all the people round the room with their heads down writing the answer.

Uncle Alan said What city is known as the Eternal City?

I knew the answer but I didnt say anything.

It was ROME.

I knew everything about Rome because it was my favourite bit of History and I had all the books from the library. I knew about Nero and the fire and the Christians and the lions. I knew that Rome began because of Romulus and Remus who were brothers and who were protected by a wolf and then found by a shepherd. I knew that Romulus was like Uncle Alan because he killed his brother and became the first King of Rome 2800 years ago.

Uncle Alan said Which popular salad gets its name from the New York hotel where it was first made?

Mum tapped her pen on the table and said Oooooooh I should know this one Im always having salads.

She went through the salads out loud. Greek salad. Tuna salad. Pasta salad. Lettuce and tomato salad.

She laughed and said I dont think theres a lettuce and tomato hotel do you Philip? I think well leave that one blank.

Mum sipped her wine and then she said Oh no. Well take a guess.

She wrote CEASAR SALAD and I saw a picture in my head of Julius Caesar with an apron on chopping a tomato and I thought how bad my brain was that it thinks stupid things even when it is planning a Murder.

Uncle Alan said Waterloo is the scene of a famous battle involving Napoleon. In which country can it be found?

Mum hummed the Waterloo song which is on her favourite CD Abba Gold and she wrote SWEDEN on the paper.

She said to me Im just nipping to the loo. And she went to the loo not the WATERLOO and I got the bottle out of my pocket and held it under the table.

Uncle Alan said Another tricky one. In which play by William Shakespeare do we find the line There is nothing either good or bad but thinking makes it so?

And I unscrewed the bottle and I waited until all the heads went down to write the answer and I poured the poison into the glass drip drip drip and I kept watching the heads and put the bottle back in my pocket. No one saw me but my heart was going like I was sprinting but I was sitting still.

Uncle Alan said Which British runner first broke the four minute mile in 1954?

I kept trying to look natural like how Leah told me you should look when you steal things but I didnt know where to look because I didnt want to look at the poisoned whisky. But I couldnt help it. It was a magnet for my eyes.

Uncle Alan said In the Bible how many loaves did Jesus need to feed the 5000?

Uncle Alan looked at the whisky on the table like he was going to drink it and he looked at his sheet of paper and he said Right two more questions in this round. Then its time for some liquid refreshment.

Two more questions and then he was going to die. It was weird. I wanted there to be more than two questions I dont know why.

He said In A Christmas Carol by Charles Dickens how many ghosts in total visited Scrooge?

When he said ghosts that is when Dads Ghost came on like a light bulb standing by the door near the toilets. He was looking at me and nodding his head like he knew Id done the poison in the glass and like he was proud I had done it.

Mum came out of the Ladies and walked straight through Dads Ghost and Uncle Alan turned round and said into the microphone And here comes my very own Christmas Carol.

Some people laughed and some people said Ahhh but Big Vic called out Pass the bucket.

Mum went red like Uncle Alan but from shyness not whisky.

She sat down and said Have I missed anything?

She looked the most happy Id ever seen her and I looked at the whisky and I felt heavy inside.

Uncle Alan said All right. This is the last question for this round.

I was hoping in my brain that it was going to be a 5000 word question that would go on for ages but the question was Which is the only river which flows both North and South of the Equator?

Then after the questions Uncle Alan said All right. Well be back in five minutes with the Music Round.

He switched the microphone off and put it back on the stand and he lifted his eyebrows up and smiled at Mum. Then he looked at the whisky and I looked at him and I looked at the whisky and I looked at Mum and he was getting closer and closer to the whisky and I went under the table and pretended to do my laces and I lifted my head and my back with all my strength like Atlas who carried the world on his back and I lifted up the table until the glasses dropped off.

Uncle Alan said Watch out!

Mum said Philip!

And I came up from under the table and the whole Pub was looking at me.

The whisky glass and the wine glass and the Pepsi glass were smashed on the floor and all the drinks were running into each other like they were rivers going into the sea and the table was wobbling but it wasnt fallen over and Uncle Alan was turning to the Pub with his hands up and he said No harm done.

And Mum said Honestly Philip.

She was standing up and wiping the white wine off her jeans like shed weed herself.

I looked at the poisoned whisky river on the floor and Uncle Alans shadow over it.

Carla came on her young legs and wiped it up.

And Dads Ghost by the toilets was shaking his head like he was ashamed of me.

He said Oh Philip. You are hopeless. Hopeless. Whats the matter with you?

Under the H

Leah was back at school the next day which was the 5th of November.

She was still coughing but she was a bit better and at first break we sat under one of the big Hs on the Rugby field. Leah was lying down on her back with her jacket over her like a duvet and she said Why were you acting mental when you came round at the weekend?

I said I dont know. Im sorry. I dont know its

She coughed in her hand and said You were well freaky.

I knew that if I didnt dare finish Leah Id never dare kill Uncle Alan and I wanted to make Dads Ghost pleased again. All I had to do was finish her but I was worried my mouth wouldnt work so I got the words ready in my head and I forced them behind my lips. My brain kept pushing until the words all fell out really fast with no spaces LeahIvegottofinishyouwecantGoOutanymore.

I didnt look at her when I said this because I didnt want to.

She sat up and said What?

I said Leah Ive got to finish you we cant Go Out any more.

She said You what?

I said Leah Ive got to fin

Her cough was gone and she said You? Youre finishing me?

I nodded my head.

She said Why? Is it because of my nose?

I said Whats the matter with your nose?

She was standing up and shaking her head and she said You cant finish me.

I said Why?

She said You cant.

I said Im sorry.

And then she picked up her coat and picked up her bag and she kicked me in the back really hard and walked away from me and back to school and I stayed under the H and watched her go smaller and smaller until she was a green and grey dot on the yard with all the other green and grey dots and she could have been a girl dot or a boy dot and I kept watching all the others all far away from me screaming and playing and laughing and it was nearly the end of the break so I wiped my eyes and said in my brain Stop crying stop crying.

The Posting

Remember remember the 5th of November people say because it was the day of the Gunpowder Plot 400 years ago in 1605 which was a long time ago when William Shakespeare who wrote Plays was alive.

Mrs Fell said the Gunpowder Plot was when a group of Catholics wanted to blow up the English Parliament and King James the First and start a Catholic Uprising so that the Catholics could make the country more fair for them.

Mrs Fell said It was very like now a days where some people try and do horrible and violent things in the name of their religion. Or because they think it is the right thing to do. Or because they believe something SO STRONGLY they dont think of anything else but their cause and they would literally kill people who dont have the same beliefs.

She looked sad when she said this and I wondered if she was thinking of her Dad Ray Goodwin.

Charlotte Wards hand went up like a firework and Mrs Fell said Yes Charlotte?

Charlotte said How did they find out about the Gunpowder Plot?

Mrs Fell said One of the men sent a letter to his brother in law who was a Member of Parliament and the letter told him not to go to Parliament on its Opening Day on November the 5th. The letter was given to other important Members of Parliament and they searched the building and found 36 barrels of gunpowder in a cellar under the House of Lords. The men waited there and arrested Guy Fawkes who was the man who was going to light the gunpowder when he entered the cellar.

Jordan Harper was in my History class and he was on the desk behind me whispering Skitso Skitso Skitso and then Helmet Helmet Helmet then Daddy? Daddy? Wheres my daddy?

He was flicking bits of rubber on me and making the Back Row laugh and Mrs Fell said Jordan is something funny? If somethings funny why dont you be kind enough and share it with the whole class? Im sure wed all like to hear it.

My face burnt hot like if Jordan said the truth my head would catch fire but Jordan said No Miss. I was just thinking about Guy Fawkes Miss. About you know what happened to him Miss.

Mrs Fell looked at me with sorry eyes and the eyes made me smaller like I was one inch tall and then she said He was made to speak to King James the First about why he wanted to kill him. And then he was tortured to make him give the names of the other men.

Jordan Harper said What kind of torture?

Mrs Fell said The rack.

Jordan Harper said Whats that?

Mrs Fell said It was a machine that pulled peoples arms and legs in opposite ways so the arms were pulled one way and the legs were pulled the other way. It was very painful.

Jordan Harper said Cool.

Mrs Fell said No. Not cool Jordan. Not cool at all. It was a very horrible and cruel form of punishment.

Jordan Harper said Did it kill him?

Mrs Fell said No. He was hung drawn and quartered along with the other men. They hung him and then cut him into quarters.

The bell went and everyone went and Mrs Fell said Are you all right Philip?

I said Yes.

She said Are you sure?

I said Yes.

Then I went outside for break.

The gold leaves of the playground came towards me whispering things like warnings and I went out and there were faces all faces everywhere Year Sevens and Year Eights but no one who wanted to talk to me now Leah my force field was gone.

I looked for Ross and Gary but I couldnt see them. It was like they were invisible. But I didnt care not having friends because friends stop you thinking in a straight line and I need to think in a straight line that stops when Uncle Alan stops. It was cold and the air was spitting rain so I went to the shelter near the Science Block but halfway I got grabbed on my back and it was Jordan Harper and Dominic Weekly and Jordan said Get his legs! Get his legs! Get him on the floor!

Dominic put out his leg behind mine and pushed me over

it in a Judo way and they were laughing and there were faces watching.

They dragged me over the wet leaves over the concrete scraping my jacket and Jordan Harper was saying Post him!

I was kicking my legs trying to get their hands off my ankles and there were no Teachers nowhere just Year Sevens and Year Eights and the black post in the shelter was getting near and the lines of faces on both sides of me were faces of giants.

Dominic and Jordan got me to the post and my jacket was up in my shoulders and my shirt was coming up. My bare back was scraping the ground and the wet grit was getting in and Agh! the post pushed in my balls and squashed them like fruit and they kept pulling my legs pushing the sicky pain like a punch up inside me.

I heard a voice over the laughing that crashed on top of me and it was a girls voice.

Get off him!

Get off him!

It was Leah and they couldnt have seen it was her because Dominic pushed her back with his elbow. That made me mad and kick my legs but this put the post more into me not just my balls but the bone now like they were going to break me in two and if I was Guy Fawkes Id have given all the names now and told on everyone.

Then Dominic let go of my left leg and I looked to see Dane and he pushed Dominic onto the floor and then he turned to Jordan and he had his fists up and said Come on hard man!

Jordan looked at Danes big square 16 year old fists and Jordan was scared and he dropped my other leg and my balls popped back out of me and I was on the floor coughing the pain out and the people were all going and Dominic lifted himself up and ran away.

Leah walked over to me but Dane grabbed her arm and he pulled her away and I coughed her name but she couldnt hear it and they walked away with Leahs straight hair blowing to me in the spitting wind.

The Bath Bomb

When I got home my back was still stinging but I was trying not to think about it. I left Mum and Uncle Alan and all the others setting up the fire and I got the box of METALLIC SODIUM out of its Hiding Place. I went to the bathroom and I locked the door and I put the box on the floor and I went to the bath and I looked at the shampoos and the bubble baths and there was a box that said Lush! Bath Bomb and I thought that was weird and I got the bottle that said

EVANESCENTS BATH SALTS

These were Uncle Alans Bath Salts that he always put in the water for his bad back and I opened the lid and I poured all the Salts down the sink and ran the tap until they were all gone.

Then I sat on the toilet on the seat. I opened the box of **METALLIC SODIUM** and all the little bits looked nearly the same as the Bath Salts so I poured them into the bottle until it

was the same level where the Bath Salts were. Then I screwed up
the top of the bottle and put it where it was by the bath and
then I went out of the bathroom and put the box of **METAL-
LIC SODIUM** back in the Hiding Place.

I went into my room and looked at the marks on my back
from the Posting. I felt some of the marks with my fingers but
some of them I couldnt reach with my hand.

I got changed into my jeans and my sweatshirt and I put my
scarf on and I put my coat on and I went downstairs and out
into the car park. There was a Bonfire and all tables outside
where Carla and Renuka were serving drinks and I saw Uncle
Alans hand rub Mums back when they were standing in front of
the fire and I saw the Guy Fawkes on the fire with his body
melting and his head melting like Gertie and the Guppies.

Mum turned and saw me like she had a sixth sense.

She said Sweetheart there you are. I wondered where youd
got to.

I said I was just changing.

She said You were a long time.

I lifted up my shoulders.

She said You missed the fire being lit.

Uncle Alan said Just in time for the fireworks. Were setting
them off at half six.

I thought in my head that Uncle Alan was going to turn
himself into a big firework the next time he had a bath. A big
tomato firework splatting all over the walls when the bath ex-
plodes KERPOW!!!!!!

I said Oh.

Mum said Theyll be good.

The big tomato said They better be bloody good the
amount they cost.

I watched his face glowing orange. His big fat face smiling at Guy Fawkes being eaten by the flames and I wondered if he will haunt me when he is a ghost and if he will try and get his Revenge and escape from the Terrors but I thought there is no one who loves him like I loved Dad. And Mum wont see him because she cant see Dads Ghost.

A man came over and it was a man in a tracksuit and it was Sleepy Eye Terry.

He said All right Alan.

Uncle Alan said Ready for kick off.

Sleepy Eye Terry said What?

Uncle Alan said Well start lighting them at half six.

Sleepy Eye Terry looked at Mum and smiled like he was nervous and I knew why he was nervous. It was because he Smashed the Pub and because he tried to strangle me and then he saw me and jumped like I was a ghost.

He said Hey up.

I didnt say anything I just walked away and I walked behind the tables and Renuka was pouring out drinks from a big bowl with a big funny spoon and she said to me Do you want some punch Philip? Theres a soft one.

I said No.

She said Isnt the fire fantastic?

She smiled a big smile in her small triangle face like she had never seen a fire before like it was three million years ago and I said Yes.

She said Its a great idea isnt it? Having a Bonfire out in the car park.

She was speaking like she was changing my nappy.

I said I dont know.

And then Les Miserable came in his navy blue leather jacket

and he asked Renuka a question in his deep down voice without moving his mouth so I went back through the people over to Mum.

Halfway there I heard a voice behind me and it said Oi Stink Bomb.

And I turned round and it was him. It was Sleepy Eye Terry and it was me who jumped now.

The Umbrella Made of Stars

I looked for Mum and Sleepy Eye Terry said Its all right. Im not a vampire. I dont bite.

I thought No but you squeeze necks like toothpaste.

I looked back at Renuka and she was pouring Les some punch and not looking at me.

Sleepy Eye Terry said I just wanted to say sorry for the other night in the park.

I said Oh.

He said Its just it was a bad night.

I said Oh.

I looked at him and he looked really sorry but that just meant he was a good actor and a good liar not a good person.

He said The Stink Bomb just pushed me over. It took blooming hours to get it out the carpet. But I flipped out. Im sorry.

And then he didnt squeeze me like toothpaste. He just walked away with his hands in his tracksuit pockets and I went

over to Mum and she said Philip whats the matter with you
tonight?

I said Nothing.

She said Why were you so rude to Terry?

I said Dont know.

She said He seems like a nice man.

Uncle Alan laughed and said Hes getting better.

Mum made a face that meant What do you mean? in face
language.

Uncle Alan said He goes to classes.

Mum said Classes?

Uncle Alan laughed and said Bit of a temper on him. Beat
up his wifes car with a baseball bat when she left him.

Baseball bat baseball bat went over in my head like an alarm
and I knew it was 100 per cent him who smashed the Pub.

Mum said What and you work with him? And go fishing?

Uncle Alan said Hes a good bloke really. He does voluntary
stuff. St Johns Ambulance.

Uncle Alan was lying to make Mum like Terry.

Hes not in St Johns Ambulance because they came to school
and he wasnt with them and even if he was in St Johns Ambulance it didnt mean anything. He still tried to squeeze the life
out of me.

Uncle Alan went and got Sleepy Eye Terry and they started
doing the fireworks. I stayed with Mum and she had her arm
round me. The fireworks were all near the Bottle Banks and I
looked for Dad but he was in the Terrors and I thought of all the
Dead Fathers watching us and I wondered if you liked fireworks
when you were a ghost.

The first firework was a Catherine Wheel that went round
and round making a weird noise. Then Uncle Alan bent down

and lit another firework and it didnt go off and he went back to it and I was saying BLOW UP BLOW UP in my head.

Mum said Be careful.

Uncle Alan stood up and ran and squinted his eyes because his back hurt and the firework went in the air and burst and made an umbrella made of stars in the sky. Everyone clapped apart from the people holding cups who went Whoo. Another firework went off which was the same but went higher up. I looked and watched the yellowy white lines of dots fade and go into the nothing night and there were five more fireworks a pink one a one that didnt go off a one like a big dandelion a one that was just a bang and a green swirly sizzly one that screamed like an animal that was hurt.

And Big Vic said in his big voice Is that it?

And Les Miserable said in his quiet and mumbly voice into his punch Cheapskate.

And some people clapped a little bit and Mum clapped a lot and then everyone started going into the Pub. Uncle Alan and Sleepy Eye Terry moved the tables and Alan said Oof my back.

That made me think he was going to have a bath tonight. But he didnt.

The Furies

Romans used to think when you died you went to the Underworld. You went over the River Styx on a ferry and went to a happy place called Hades. But you could only go if you had been buried properly because if you werent buried properly with no coin in your mouth the ferryman called Charon wouldnt let you cross the river. So your dead body would just stay on the river till dogs came to eat it up. There were nasty angels called Furies who watched all the dead bodies and they laughed and liked seeing all the blood because most of the people who werent buried had died bad deaths. Some had been CRUCIFIED and some had got their heads chopped off or their throats cut and some like the Christians had been chomped by lions but the Furies liked seeing all the blood because they thought the bodies deserved it and it made them feel happy for being angels not humans because angels are better than humans and ghosts and they dont feel pain.

Time Machine

I woke up and it was still dark. There was a sound of a train far away and it was like the world was doing a sigh. Sometimes when you wake up you are in a different time like you have gone in a time machine and the time I was in was before Dad died.

Everything was normal and Dad was in bed with Mum in the next room sleeping with his arm flopped over her and I was thinking about going to see Derby with him on Saturday. It was going to be good and my thinking was getting faster and less sleepy and pushing me through time until I was in this morning.

Then I knew Dad wasnt in the next room and he was not taking me to the Football and when I remembered a heavy feeling came into my brain.

In the future there will probably be scales that can weigh how heavy memories are and it will be like when Mum and

Renuka went to Weightwatchers. People or special doctors at Brainwatchers will say This memory is very heavy you need to lose weight in your brain.

Then they will tell you to exercise your brain in the right way to make it lighter.

My brain was so heavy this morning I didnt think I would be able to get it off the pillow without shaking out some of the pictures in my head of Dad. Like the picture of him when he flicked water on me and Mum when he was in the swimming pool in Rhodes and we were dry on the sunbeds.

Or the heavier picture of him when it was Christmas Day and the Pub was closed and he was wearing his orange paper crown and he cried at Titanic and said Im not crying dont be daft Im not crying but he was.

Or when we went to see Derby and we had to hide our scarves because we were sitting with all the Away fans.

Or the heaviest picture of all which was when we went to Sconce Hills in the snow and his face was red and cold but his hands were warm in his woolly pattern gloves and I was still little enough not to be scared of holding his hand and he was dragging the sledge.

He was looking down at me and his words made clouds in the air and snowflakes turned into rain on his nose and his words said Come on Ill race you to the top.

And he let go of my hand and ran up the hill and even though he was pulling the sledge I didnt catch him. But then he slowed down at the top and let me run past. And when I ran past him he said like on the TV And Philip Noble in lane seven comes straight from behind and takes his place in the History books with a new World Record.

And then when we were at the top we both crunched onto

the snow on our backs and laughed clouds up to the sky and I sat on my elbows and looked at him lying in the snow and felt the most happy ever but then I cant remember anything else because the picture is snow and melts in my brain.

The Real Uncle Alan

I heard water running like a waterfall. It was the bath. It was
Uncle Alan having his bath.

Then my brain went click like Lego and I remembered his
exploding Bath Salts and I wondered if it would explode the
whole Pub or just in the bathroom. I thought it would just be in
the bathroom because the walls were thick and the bath was
thin and Uncle Alan was soft.

And I just stayed lying in bed holding my breath and trying
to stop me from stopping Uncle Alan getting in the bath.

The water was still running and there was a voice coming
out of the bathroom and it wasnt Alan it was just saying Alan.

Alan.

Alan.

Alan.

Alan.

Alaaaan!

I thought Oh no but then I thought Its OK because Mum

doesnt have a bad back and then I heard Alan in Mums bedroom and he said What?

And Mum said Shall I put your Bath Salts in?

And it wasnt Mums bath. She was running Uncle Alans bath for him like he was a King and she was a Slave and I thought Oh no because she was about to blow herself up.

Uncle Alan said If youd be so kind.

I jumped out of bed and ran to the bathroom and tried to open the door but it wouldnt open and I banged on it and Uncle Alan said behind me What the hell?

I said Mum.

Mum!

Mum!

Mum!

Mum!

Mum!

I kept trying the handle and banging on the wood with my hand and then I banged with my feet and they were bare feet but I didnt feel them hurt.

I said Mum dont use the Salts! Dont use the Salts! Dont put them in the water!

Mum turned off the tap and she said through the door Philip?

I said Open the door Mum open the

She was standing there with the green towel on her like a dress with her bare shoulders and her bare legs. She was holding the Bath Salts with the top screwed on and I grabbed them out of her hand and she said Philip? What on Earth are you doing?

After I grabbed the Bath Salts that werent Bath Salts I held them onto my chest like I was holding a Rugby ball and I heard Mums voice chasing me.

Philip?

Philip?
Philip?
Philip?
Philip?

And I was in my pyjamas and in my bare feet and I ran down the stairs and down the hall past the office. I opened the back door and I ran out into the car park with my feet hurting on the little bits of stones that were on the ground and I went right over to the Bottle Banks and put them in the Green Bottle Bank. I ran quickly away because the glass smashed and there was water and wine inside the Bottle Bank and I thought it would explode like in a film with a big fireball and a black smoke cloud but it didnt it just started making pings and smashes.

Ping!
Smash!
Ping!
Smash!
Ping!
Smash!
Ping!
Smash!

And it was weird like all the glass for Recycling had made some mad glass creature alive inside the Bottle Bank that wanted to escape but couldnt break through the metal. After a bit the creature called the Glassman gave up and there were no more noises out of the Bottle Bank.

I was standing still in the car park now and I heard a Beep!

It was Carla and her hoop earrings in her little white car with the headlights still on and she was frowning through the windscreen but not in a cross way.

And I looked at her and I lifted my hand in a wave and I

went over the tarmac to the back door and Uncle Alan was there in his dressing gown and his ENGLAND GLORY T shirt underneath but you could only see the AND and he said What you doing son?

I said Er for ages.

I said Er Er Er recycling.

The real Uncle Alan inside the pretend Uncle Alan said in an angry voice What?

I was scared but Carla was shutting her car door and coming over and this made the real Uncle Alan hide again and the pretend Uncle Alan smiled at Carla and her earrings and he said All right love.

Carla said Hiya duck.

She looked at me and my bare feet and Uncle Alan said Kids.

Carla smiled and thought of Ross and Gary and said You dont have to tell me.

And then there was a tinkle sound right next to my feet. A little bit of green glass had pinged out of the Bottle Bank. Uncle Alan looked at me and I lifted my shoulders.

I went inside and upstairs and Mum was on the top of the stairs in her towel and she said Philip whats got into you? And what have you done with Uncle Alans Bath Salts?

I said I dont know.

She said What do you mean you dont know?

I said I thought it was empty. I put it in the Bottle Bank.

She said Philip why are you doing this to me?

I said Im not doing anything.

She said Why are you making it so hard? Is it because of your fish?

Uncle Alan came up the stairs after speaking to Carla and Mum started sniffing up tears.

Uncle Alan said to me Do you see what youre putting your mother through lad?

The real me inside the pretend me came out and said Its your fault! Its all your fault!

And I went into my room and shut my door and left Mum crying into Uncle Alans dressing gown.

Daddy Long Legs

Dad told me Daddy long legs which are crane flies are the most poisonous animals in the world but they never kill anyone because they cant poison anyone without teeth and they have no teeth. So if all the other animals pick on them and shout Oi long legs! they cant do anything. They can say Im very poisonous and it is true but the other animals wont believe them because they never poison anyone. They know they could kill and go up the FOOD CHAIN if they had teeth but they dont because God forgot. I dont know if this is true or not.

Pocket Money

Mrs Fell over Mrs Fell in love Mrs Fell down a cliff Mrs Fell a tree Mrs Fell tip pen was sitting in her chair and she said You can talk to me Philip. You can tell me anything.

I said I know Miss.

She said Anything at all.

I said I know.

She said Is there anything youd like to tell me?

I said Like what?

She said Like anything. Like what you are thinking right now.

I was thinking about how Ray Goodwin was murdered so I said Im not thinking anything.

She said How are you going to spend the weekend?

I said I dont know.

She said Are you going to do anything interesting?

I lifted the question up on my shoulders.

She said If you could do anything this weekend what would you like to do?

I said I cant.

She said Cant what.

I said I cant do anything.

She said I know. But if you could do anything. Anything at all. What would it be? How would you like to spend your time?

Mrs Fell always says things like this. She is nice but she doesnt understand some things. She doesnt know that time is not like pocket money that you can spend because time is the person spending the pocket money and the pocket money is you.

I said If I could do anything?

She said Yes. If you could do anything in the world.

I said Anything?

She said Anything at all.

I said Id go to Rhodes with my mum and dad.

Her smile got more stretched on every word and then it snapped back when I said Dad.

She said Yes Philip. Yes. All right. Yes. But your dad

I said My dads dead.

She said Yes Philip yes he is.

I said And I cant bring him back.

She closed her eyes and said in a soft voice No. No Philip Im afraid you cant.

I said But you said anything.

She said Yes yes I did.

I thought Mrs Fell was feeling bad so I said Id like to go to Rome as well.

She smiled again and said Rome?

I said Id like to go to the Circus Maximus and see the chariots.

She said I dont think they still do the chariot racing.

I said I know I mean Id like to go to Ancient Rome. In a time machine.

She said Oh.

I said Id go to the Colosseum and see the Gladiators.

She said It might get a bit violent.

I said Id like to see the Retiarii.

She said Which ones are they?

I said Theyre the ones with nets like fishermen and big forks.

She said You like History dont you Philip?

I said Its my favourite subject.

I wanted to say that Mrs Fell was my favourite Teacher but I didnt.

She said Its mine too.

I said Everythings History.

She said Yes.

I said Did you always want to be a Teacher?

She said in a sad voice Not always. No.

I said What did you want to be?

She said Oh all sorts of things.

I said Like what?

She sighed and said An actress.

I said Youd be a good actress.

She smiled and a twinkle went on in her eyes and she said Why? Why do you think that?

I said Because youre pretty.

I said it just like that not thinking. And then it was out of my head and inside the room in the pot of marker pens and coming out of the computer and on the papers on her desk.

Because youre pretty because youre pretty because youre pretty.

And my cheeks went red and the red was catching and Mrs Fell caught it.

She said Well I dont know about that. But Im sure flattery will get you everywhere Philip.

I had to say something. I had to say anything at all to rub out Because youre pretty and so I said My fish melted.

She said What?

I said My tropical fish melted. The water was too hot.

She said Oh Philip thats terrible. Im so sorry.

I said What for?

And she said Im sorry about what happened to your fish.

I dont know why people say sorry when they havent done the thing they are saying sorry for. It is like everyone in the world is a little bit to blame for everything.

I said It was my uncle Alan.

She said Oh Philip Im sure it

I said He turned up the heater.

She said Did you see him turn up the heater Philip?

I said No. But I know it was him.

She said Im sure whatever happened it was an accident. Life is full of accidents Philip. Thats one of the biggest lessons of History.

History.

Fishtory.

I said Not if youre religious.

She said What?

I said If youre religious then everythings Gods fault.

She said Well I

I said Do you think thats why Emperor Nero blamed the Christians?

She said Emperor Nero?

I said For the fire in Rome.

She said I dont know. I dont think so Philip.

I said I think so Miss. I think thats why.

I thought it was weird that Mrs Fell thought everything was an accident because Ray Goodwin her dad was murdered but I thought Mrs Fell is not a normal type of person.

And then I said Have you ever done anything bad? That you did on purpose?

She looked at me and drank me with her eyes and she waited a long time and she said Yes Philip yes.

I was going to ask what it was that she did and I think she would have said but I didnt ask her because I still wanted to believe in the Mrs Fell in my head so I didnt say anything at all.

Emperor Nero and Emperor Neros Mum

I am scared of what will happen to me if I kill Uncle Alan.

I am not scared of getting found out because I will be clever and make it look like an accident but I am scared of doing more bad things.

Once you do one bad thing everything changes and you end up doing more bad things like Emperor Nero.

I read about Emperor Nero in a book from the library in school on the Romans and it said Emperor Nero started off quite nice. He had a Teacher called Seneca but he probably had to call him Mr Seneca.

Emperor Neros mum was weird.

She married her uncle Emperor Claudius who was old and dribbled a lot and she married him and then killed him with poisoned mushrooms just so Nero could be Emperor.

Nero was still a boy when he was Emperor.

He was good in the beginning because he listened to his Teacher Mr Seneca who was good and didnt like there being

Slaves even when everyone else did. But his mum was always there hiding behind curtains and getting Nero to do what she wanted.

Nero was still good for a bit and he tried to stop the Games which was where the Gladiators killed each other but everyone loved the Games so he couldnt stop it. He had to do other things instead like put criminals to death. He didnt like doing it but he got more and more used to it and once he had to kill hundreds of Slaves just because one Slave had murdered his master because that was the law. After he did that he became bad.

He put poison in some cake at a childs birthday party so he could kill his brother who was BRITANNICUS who might have wanted to be an Emperor. And killing is like Pringles which are Mums favourite crisps. Once you pop you cant stop.

So Nero killed his wife because he wanted to marry another woman who was very pretty called Poppaea and I think this might be like Uncle Alan because Uncle Alan fancies Carla the Barmaid. I have seen him touch her bum when he walks past her behind the bar to get some crisps. They are not Pringles they are McCoys cheddar flavour and make his breath smell even worse than normal.

Uncle Alan might kill Mum to marry Carla the Barmaid and then he might kill Carla the Barmaid because Emperor Nero went POP and killed Poppaea. He kicked her in the head when he was cross.

And now Emperor Nero was older and he didnt have any good left in him. It had all run out and so he killed lots of Christians after the fire. Then he had to keep killing to stay the Emperor and did the most bad thing which was kill his mum.

His mum was cross with Nero and Nero had a big argument with his mum but then PRETENDED to Make Up with her and invited her to a party and she said Yes Ill go to the party.

She had to go to the party on a boat so Nero built a special boat which was meant to fall apart in the middle of the sea and make her drown. But the boat didnt sink it just broke. When the men on the boat tried to make it sink Neros mums best friend PRETENDED to be Neros mum and said Save me Im Neros mum!!!

Neros mums friend was very brave because she knew they were going to kill her and they did. They smashed her with their oars which rowed the boat.

The real Neros mum escaped and she wrote Nero a letter which said There was a boat accident but Im alive dont worry!!!

And Emperor Nero went mad and sent two men to her and they PRETENDED they were seeing if she was all right.

They said Are you all right?

And Neros mum said Yes.

Then one man got out a big wooden stick like a baseball bat and started beating her up. Then the other man pulled out his sword and she knew it was Nero who tried to kill her so she lifted up her clothes and showed her stomach and pointed to it and said Stab me here because this is where Nero came from.

They said OK.

And they stabbed her and Nero said to everyone She killed herself.

He pretended to be sad like Uncle Alan pretended to be sad when Dad died.

And now Nero didnt trust anyone not even Mr Seneca who he made kill himself. But no matter how many people Nero killed he was never safe. And this is because killing is not a stone you throw away it is a boomerang that comes back and gets you on the head.

In the end Neros own soldiers wanted to get rid of him and

they went to get Nero so Nero killed himself but not properly so one of the soldiers finished killing him.

And in the book I got from the library it says at the bottom of the page

> When Nero was born, an astrologer predicted: 'He will be Emperor and he will kill his mother.'

And he was Emperor and he did kill his mum. I dont know what an ASTROLOGER said when I was born but it is really mad that everything that is going to happen might be in the stars right now and I cant change it and Uncle Alan cant change it and no one can change it. Not even Mum who always reads the stars in her magazines and she used to say Its going to be a good week this week. Says so here.

She said it every week and she said it on the week Dad died in the crash so the stars must keep some things secret and not let the magazines know. And the secrets about my future are written now in the sky and I cant change them I cant change anything even these words and this full stop.

The Condom Machine

Dads Ghost does not like the way Uncle Alan has changed the Pub. Dads Ghost does not like the fruit machines and the game of Who Wants to be a Millionaire? Or the Karaoke or the Pub Quiz or the Machine in the toilets.

Dads Ghost only says the Machine. He doesnt say its full name which is the Condom Machine because he must think I dont know what a condom is. A condom is what men put on their willies if they dont want to have babies. They are also used to make water bombs and Dominic Weekly put one over his head at Hadrians Wall and blew it up until it burst.

It is weird that Dads Ghost thinks the word CONDOM is more dangerous than killing Uncle Alan but that is what makes me think Dads Ghost is really still Dad. The Machine has different types of condoms like RIBBED and TEXTURED and FRUIT FLAVOURS and VARIETY PACK which has CURRY FLAVOUR.

Condom is a weird word.

Condom.

Condom.

Condom.

Condom.

It is a bit like kingdom which is a land ruled by kings so a condom is a land ruled by cons!!!!!

A con is a lie.

The Ticking Clocks

I was going to kill Uncle Alan at the weekend because I had a new plan but I forgot I was going to Sunderland with Mum. So I had to wait until after which was OK because it was only one night and there was still some of the No Time left because Dads Birthday was miles away.

Sunderland is the worst part of England. It is where Mum comes from and where Nan lives. Mum always tells Nan to move near Newark but she doesnt want to. She wants to stay living in Sunderland and Mum always says Youre scared to go out of your house.

Nan says Its the same all over.

Mum says No Mam its not.

Nan says Anyhow I cant leave George.

George is Grandad and he died in 2002 on September the 10th but Nan always talks like he is still alive but she knows hes dead really.

Nan always loves me. I dont know why. I dont do anything. I just sit and eat biscuits. But she always smiles at me like sitting down and eating biscuits is a special trick.

It was Saturday and we got to her door at 11:00 and she opened the door at 11:05 and she gave me a hairy kiss.

Mum was a shoe done up tight with a double knot and it was because she was scared of telling Nan about Uncle Alan.

And Mum didnt talk about Uncle Alan at first. She talked about all the shops and houses near Nans house which are dead with wood over all the windows and Nan said Its the same all over.

Nan makes the days longer in her house. She checks to make sure with a clock. The clock is on a shelf over the fire. It is a round circle with Roman Numerals and gold round it and it is in a stand which is the shape of a grave. It is white and it has flowers and plants and butterflies painted on it and it goes TICK TOCK TICK TOCK all day but it is the slowest clock in the world and it stays 20 minutes past 12 for half an hour.

Nan does nothing all day just her cross stitch and her cross word and her cross face when she watches the news or the window when girls go by with babies.

Then when it was still 20 minutes past 12 Mum said about getting married to Uncle Alan and Nan laughed like it was a joke. But Nan never laughs so I think she knew it was real.

Mum said Mam Im being serious.

Nan said Oh aye pet of course.

Mum said Mam please. Listen. Were getting married.

Nan coughed over Mums words and said Its all on my chest. It wont come up.

She got a tissue out. She put it to her mouth and put gob and greenies in it. There was spit strings from her mouth to the tissue like wires on cable cars and then the strings snapped and went on the tissue and then she said Sorry pet?

Mum said Alans asked me to marry him and Ive said Yes.

Nan said nothing and then she said Never in the world.

Mum said Now I know what youre thinking.

Nan said Im not thinking anything.

Mum said You think its too soon.

Nan said A month? Why no.

Mum said Two months. Its been two months.

Nan said Well then two months. Why Im surprised you even remember your Brians name after two months.

Mum said Mam please.

Nan said Thats plenty of time for Brian to turn in his grave. And anyhow it makes perfect sense marrying his brother. I mean you wont even have to change your name.

Nan looked at me and then at Mum and her eyes went sharp and she said Youre going to do that to the poor lad?

Mum said Do what?

Nan said I feel heart sorry for the poor bairn.

I was a bairn now. I was a man after the funeral but I was a bairn now.

Mum said Mam dont.

Nan said His dad dies then you take up with his uncle I mean what are you trying to do to him?

Mum said Philip go and play in the yard.

I looked out of the glass windows in the patio and the white lines of the blind straight down like prison bars.

The yard is nothing and has nothing in it. Not even one ball. It looked cold and I looked at the sky with big clouds like brains and I said Its cold.

Nan looked at my T shirt and said He needs more than a T shirt in this weather.

Mum said Hes got a jacket.

Nan said Oh that flimsy thing. You might as well put him in a bin liner as make him wear that.

Mum said Its not as cold in Newark.

Nan said Oh aye. Youre practically at the pyramids in Newark. The Trent joins up with the Nile.

Mum said Philip go in the spare bedroom just for a minute while I talk to your nan.

So I went in the spare bedroom which is on the same floor because all of Nans house is on the same floor. It is a BunGaLow because Nan cant climb stairs because of her hip which is made of metal. The metal is called TITanium and if you got a really big magnet youd be able to get Nan to fly to it even if you put the magnet next to the wall and she was in the other room youd be able to get her to stick to the wall in the other room. If the magnet was high up it would lift her off the ground and she would be stuck to the wall and not be able to reach anything because the walls are thin like paper. Big white sheets of paper.

Nans metal hip makes her walk with a twisty face because it hurts. She has two metal walking sticks so she walks like she has four long legs like she is a crane fly on the water. She has a bad back as well.

She has ost something osis.

This means her back is like a question mark and she is shrinking. She used to be tall and now she is the same as me and one day we might come and Mum will say Wheres Nan gone?

She will be there on the carpet one centimetre tall saying Help help help Im shrinking and we might lose her again and Mum will say Wheres Nan gone now? And Ill check my shoes and Nan will be on my shoe stuck in my chewing gum going Help me help me Im stuck in the chewing gum.

Tick Tock Tick Tock

Mums voice was getting louder and her words came out of the paper wall in whole pieces and they were Do you think its been easy for me? Its been terrible. Youve no idea. Brian left everything in a mess. I had no idea how much money he had borrowed. And how much the Pub was losing. He never bloody told me. And Ive had to deal with all this bank stuff on top of everything else. Philip getting into all sorts of trouble at school. Worrying me to death the way hes been going on. And Alans been so nice and hes been so kind and helped us out with money and

And then her words were getting quieter again and only coming out broken in half pieces ip ot ans ted ing and I couldnt mend them.

I tried to listen but there was another clock by the spare bed tick tock. It was next to the picture of Grandad which didnt look like Grandad because he was young and all grey. It was an old photograph of old times when everything was grey and smart and his eyes looked sad like he knew his future. Like he knew he was going to end up on the sofa all the time getting thinner because he couldnt eat without being sick.

And in between the clock tick tocking Mum was crying. She was always crying all the time now. I didnt know if the crying was about me or money or Dad. It was about me I think.

I looked out the window and there was nothing just the wall of Next Door.

I felt weird and I said Hello.

I dont know why I just wanted to hear my voice to check I was real but it didnt sound like my voice and the clock was getting louder TICK TOCK TICK TOCK and I got on the bed and lay down and the ceilings swervy circles started spinning round and my skin itched and things you dont think about like breathing in and out I was thinking about like if I stopped thinking about it Id stop breathing and the air was different air like Coke is different to Pepsi it was Cocacola air not Pepsi air and I said Hello again but my voice was still a long way from me.

My heart was doing its funny beating with no stops in it and I thought why am I me why am I not Mum why am I not the ticking clock why am I not a fish why am I not a loaf of bread why am I alive and most people are dead how do I know Im me how do I know Im alive and I thought it must be good to be dead not dead like Dads dead but to be nothing like when you sleep but then I thought it might be a bad sleep with lots of nightmares like the one I had last night when I was trapped in the black box and then my hand started shaking and I was scared why my hand was shaking and I thought I was going to die and I said Mum! Mum! Mum!

Mum came in and opened the door and her eyes were red and she looked at me and said Philip whats the matter?

And far away my voice said I dont know. I feel weird. I dont know my hands shaking.

And she came and felt my head and my heart and sat on the bed next to me and said Its OK its OK Philip youre just in a bit of a panic its OK.

And Nan was a crane fly in the door with her silver front legs and she was saying Dinny chew yourself up lad and Mum said Deep breaths Philip and I said Am I going to die? And she said No which was a lie but I think she meant Not right now and she said Now come on deep breaths and I sucked the Coca-cola air in big gulps and still felt empty and the clock was just getting louder

tick

tock

tick

Going Home

We were on the motorway going home and Mum said Well go to the Doctors tomorrow after school OK? Well take you to see Dr Crawford tomorrow. OK Philip OK?

We went for one mile which was one minute and then I said Yes OK.

And the motorway went on for ever and Mum said Were going to be late. Id better text Nooks and say Ill be too late for the gym.

Mum got the phone out of her left boob pocket and did the text with one hand and the steering wheel with the other hand with her eyes going phone road phone road.

And I thought we could die now we could crash into the barriers and be in a Pile Up and I liked that thought.

I looked out of the window at the 60 miles an hour grass melting past and the other cars going nearly the same speed and Mums car walked past them and we passed a lorry and the driver looked down at me when we went by and then we passed a car and there were two girls two twins in the back but little girls like they were eight.

They waved at me out of the window.

I just looked at them until they stopped waving and then I looked at the dad and the mum in the front seats and they were laughing and the mum was turning round to the twin girls and the dad was saying something. I dont know what he was saying but it was a nice thing like Do you want to go to the Little Chef?

And I looked at the dad and he was wearing a Polo Neck and he had a beard like Emperor Hadrian who had a scar on his face. That is why he had a beard and I wondered if the man had a scar on his face and I wondered if he went Trick or Treating. He saw me looking at him out of the window and I smiled and he smiled at me and I wondered if he would fancy Mum.

I thought he might do. Mum was prettier than the mum in the car. Mum is not as pretty as Mrs Fell but Mrs Fell is the most pretty woman in England probably.

The dad and mum and twins car was turning off now and the man was never going to meet Mum and fall in love with her and kiss her lips and save her from Uncle Alan.

It was not day and not night now it was a mix and we passed a sign that said Newark 42 and Mum said Lets have some music.

She switched on the radio and it was a song and the woman singing had a voice like a duvet that goes round you and warms you up and I looked at Mum and she had tears shining in her eyes and one tear went down her face rubbing out her Make Up and I said Why are you crying? because I wanted to know why she was crying.

And Mum wiped the tear and went in the Slow Lane and said I dont know Philip please I dont know.

I looked out of the window at the purple clouds in the sky going dark and I closed my eyes and the man like Emperor Hadrian was opening his front door and smiling at his dog and rubbing his hand on the dogs head and the twins ran in the house.

Diazepam

I dont like Dr Crawford.

He is the doctor who made me get my willy half chopped off in the Summer Holidays before Dad died because the skin was too tight when it was thinking about girls. I had to go to hospital and I had to have injections and go to sleep with a nurse counting backwards ten nine eight seven sleep. After the operation I woke up and it was all white like in Heaven but there was pain and I looked inside my pyjamas and there were big stitches like thorns. It wasnt good because I had to walk like a hunchback and not let it touch my pyjama bottoms so I had to hold the elastic really far out like I had an invisible fat stomach. When I went to new school it was still a bit sore but the stitches were out. They just fell out when I used to pick them when I went for wees. In the first week of the new school I had to do Games and it was Rugby so Mr Rosen made us shower. After that Dominic and Jordan called me Helmet because it looks like a helmet on a Roman soldier and Jew Nob and I didnt know why and Dad said Jews have to be Circumsized as well and I said Why? and he didnt know why.

Dr Crawford has glasses. I dont know why he has glasses because he looks over them all the time with his chin in his neck. And Dr Crawford is old. He has lines all over his face like he is a map you cant understand and he said to Mum So whats the matter?

Mum said about my heart beating really fast and my sleep walking and my breathing and my shaking sometimes and my other things and Dr Crawford kept looking at me over his glasses and sitting in his chair with his long crossed legs and nodding fast at Mums words like the words were food and he was a bird eating them.

And when Mum had finished talking Dr Crawford said These are all classic signs of a Panic Disorder which in this case has probably been triggered by the circumsizes of his fathers death.

I dont know if the word was circumsizes but that was what it sounded like.

Mum said Oh.

And he turned his long flamingo legs under his desk and started writing on paper and Mum said Will he be all right?

Dr Crawford said Yes. Im sure hell be all right Mrs Noble. Its just a case of controlling his nervous system and controlling the ADRENALIN that is causing his heart rate to increase.

Mum said I see. So what are they? I mean the pills. Theyre not erm

Dr Crawford said Theyre called DIAZEPAM.

Mum said Are they. You know. Are they. I mean are they OK for children?

Dr Crawford said In the doses I shall be advising yes it is perfectly suitable for children of Philips age.

And Dr Crawford handed Mum the paper and Mum looked at the writing but didnt understand doctor language because only Chemists understand doctor language so she took me over the road to the Chemist and got me the tablets and she said Youll be better now Philip. Youll be right as rain.

Hello.
Hello.
Hello.
Hello.
Hello.
Hello.
Hello.
Hello.
Hello.
Hello.
Hello.
Hello.
Hello.
Hello.
Hello.
Hello.
Hello.
Hello.
Hello.
Hello.
Hello.
Hello.
Hello.
Hello.

Watching TV with Mum

I was in the Living Room with Mum on the settee. She wasnt working behind the bar because she wanted to make sure I was OK. She said in a whisper Have you had your third tablet?

I said Yes.

Uncle Alan was asleep on Dads chair in his blue Garage uniform and he was sleeping like a radio in between the stations sometimes saying words I couldnt hear sometimes nose whistling.

I watched the news with Mum.

Mum didnt like the news. She liked watching Famous People eating insects in the jungle. The news was just on because the remote control was under Uncle Alan and Uncle Alan was asleep.

On TV there was a bomb in IRAQ going off and people were dead. Children and grown ups and other people were running with blood on their faces and crying and screaming at the screen like at us. There was a man who was not screaming and he said The people here on the streets of this city are beginning to fear they are caught in an endless cycle of violence.

Mum held my hand and said Its a horrible world.

And I didnt say anything. I just let my head fall on her shoulder and I could smell Mums hair and her shampoo which is Herbal Essences and it was nice. She kissed the top of my head and I wished it was just me and Mum not Uncle Alan making radio noises and my eyes were tired and the TV was going smudgy like the screen was leaking into the room so the colours of IRAQ were mixing with the red carpet in long thin lines like when Dads Ghost comes.

And I said quiet into her shirt and into her boobs Dont marry him.

But Mum couldnt hear so I said it again Dont marry Uncle Alan.

Mum heard this time and she pushed me off her shoulder and said in a shout whisper Philip stop this. Please stop this.

I said Mum dont go to bed with him. Please Mum dont. He killed.

And then I said it without thinking.

He killed Dad.

And Mum just looked at me and I had made tears in her eyes for the 200th time and she said still whispering but crying Philip why are you being like this? Why are you doing this to me? Why are you saying these horrible things? Why wont you stop Philip? Its endless Philip. Endless.

And I think endless was in her head because the news man said it because she never says endless ever.

I said Dads Ghost comes and sees me and he says Uncle Alan was

And Mum spoke over my words and said Philip stop it. Philip stop it. You have to stop it Philip or theyll take you away

Philip. Theyll take you away if you talk about seeing ghosts and if you keep smashing things up Philip. Please Philip. Just try Philip. For me. For me Philip. For me.

And then she stopped talking and stopped crying and wiped her eyes and smudged black on her face from her Make Up because Uncle Alan was waking up and reaching his station and rubbing his lips together and wiping his face with his car engine hands.

Uncle Alan looked at the TV and said Is it still the bloody news?

Mum said Yes it is yes.

Uncle Alan said Have you told him?

I felt Mums body pull its laces.

Mum said No.

Then Mum said We can do it on the 22nd.

I said What?

She said Theres been a cancellation.

I looked at the running people on the screen and they were still screaming.

She said At the Registry Office.

Uncle Alan said Isnt that great?

And I looked at him but the Anger Switch in my brain wasnt working. I kept trying and trying to press it but the only thing I was feeling was tired so I didnt do anything. I just fell asleep on Mums shoulder.

die die die die die die die die die die
die die die die die die die die die
die die die die die die die die
die die die die die die die
die die die die die die
die die die die die
die die die die
die die die
die die
die

The Ticking Days

Tick tock tick tock tick tock tick went the time before the Wedding and Dads Ghost kept telling me to kill Uncle Alan but I didnt know how and my brain was going slower than normal.

I had an idea of putting the rest of the Metallic Sodium in the sugar bowl because Uncle Alan had five sugars in his tea and the mug would be a bomb and explode in his face.

But then I thought this was a bad idea because Mum sometimes made his tea for him and even when she didnt make his tea she was sometimes in the kitchen with him when he made his tea and she sometimes puts sugar on her Special K so I am going to have to find another way to kill Uncle Alan.

But the days kept tick tock ticking and Dads Ghost said Its the tablets son. Theyre slowing you down. Theres less than a month until the No Time is over. Its 29 days until the 10th of December. 29 days. Even less till the Wedding.

I said I know.

He said Stop taking the tablets Philip. Stop taking them. Theyre making you weak.

Tick tock tick tock tick tock

Theyre making you

Week seven six five four three two one

I said They make me feel better.

Dads Ghost said Stop taking them son. Please. Stop taking them.

Tick tock tick tock tick tock went the days and then I woke up and it was the Wedding morning the 22nd of November.

Mum came into my bedroom and said Have you taken your tablet?

And I said Yes.

But it was a lie.

The Drips and the Drops
and the Windsor Knot

Uncle Alan had been in the bath. I could smell his new Salts and I could smell his poo in the toilet. I went in the bath and I just lay there and I wasnt thinking anything I was just listening to the tap go drip drop drip drop drip drop drop.

I kept hearing the voices of Mum and Uncle Alan between the drips and the drops and Uncle Alan was saying I dont scrub up bad if I do say so myself.

Mum said Are my shoes OK? Theyre not too much with the dress? Theyre not too high? Do I look all right?

And Uncle Alan said Like a movie star. Like a magazine.

And then Uncle Alan went past the door and down the stairs whistling what hed been whistling all week.

The whistle was Im getting married in the morning ding dong the bells are going to drip drop drip drop drip drop drip drip drip drop.

And Mum said behind the door Philip love. Philip? Philip? And I said What?

And she said Weve got to be at the Registry Office half an hour early Philip. How are you getting on?

And I said All right.

And Mum said Ill just go and sort Nan out.

And I stayed in a bit more until the water was cold like the coldest Roman bath which is the Frigidarium which is where Romans went after the Tepidarium warm bath and the Calidarium hot bath and then I got out and dried my body and dried my head under the towel and I liked it under the towel. It was like another world. Like a green towel world that was soft.

Uncle Alan was four hours on the motorway just him and Nan the night before. Nan hates him and Uncle Alan hates Nan but human beings always hate each other and pretend they dont. That is what being a human being is about.

I went out of the bathroom in my green towel like a skirt and I went into my bedroom.

Mum had got my suit out and it was the same suit I had for Dads funeral but with a light white shirt not a dark blue shirt. I looked at the suit on the bed and it looked weird like someone had run over me with a steam roller or turned me flat like paper.

Mum was talking to Nan downstairs but I couldnt hear the words. I put the suit on. I tucked the shirt in after I put the jacket on and that made it hard. My brain was still a bit slow from the tablets but it was speeding up. Then I put the tie on and when I was putting the tie on I wasnt looking in the mirror I was looking at air that had been water where the fish had been melted.

And I saw Gertie swimming in the air. Just Gertie on her own swimming. I tried to touch her but there was nothing there and I went out of the room and stood on the top of the stairs and Uncle Alan was coming up the stairs in elephant steps and he said All right lad?

I said Yes.

He was wearing his tight suit with his neck pouring out.

He said Shall I sort your tie out son?

I said What?

He said Your ties all wonky.

I said Oh.

He said Shall I do you a knot like mine?

I looked at Uncle Alans knot. It was a small triangle upside down and he said Its a Windsor knot.

I said I dont know.

He said Its a special Wedding knot.

I didnt want him to do me a Windsor knot but his big hands were already on my tie and he was undoing it and then he lifted my collars up and I thought he might squeeze the life out of me like Sleepy Eye Terry wanted to and Mum and Nan wouldnt hear. But he didnt.

I saw Dads Ghost on the stairs behind Uncle Alan and I was on the top stair and Uncle Alan was two steps down so I could see over his shoulder and Dads Ghost said Now is the time Philip.

I said What?

Uncle Alan was putting the tie through the knot and he said I didnt say anything.

Dads Ghost said This is your moment Philip. Push him down the stairs Philip. Push with all your strength son.

I said I I I

Uncle Alan said Are you all right son?

Dads Ghost said Kill him kill him now Philip. Before he marries her.

I said I dont want to.

Uncle Alan said Ive nearly finished it now lad.

Dads Ghost said Do it Philip. Do it before its too late.

And I closed my eyes and lifted up my hands and my Dads Ghost said Push him Philip. Push him.

And I was going to push him. I was going to do it. But I heard Mum at the bottom of the stairs and she said Whos that handsome man?

The Wedding

I opened my eyes and Uncle Alan finished off the tie and Dads Ghost wasnt there any more and Mum was wearing a light green dress and two light green shoes and her hair was in slides like it was going inside her head and her face had Make Up on and her eyebrows were like wings of birds when you draw them flying in the sky and her pink lips made her teeth pink as well.

She looked at me and the me she was seeing wasnt the real me who nearly killed Uncle Alan because she was smiling like I was a magic boy. Her eyes were shiny with more tears in them and Nan was there behind with her four legs on the carpet that was blue like a pond.

Nan looked up at me and said Ee what a picture.

Uncle Alan went past me and went into the toilet and shut the door and he started to wee elephant wee.

Mum was two people now. A moving fast person inside a moving slow person. Or a moving slow person inside a moving fast person. I dont know which.

And she said Philip could you start taking Nan to the car?

And then she said Keys keys keys.

I went down the stairs and held onto Nans elbow and her baggy skin with no blood inside it and Nan made a noise like she was hurt just by me touching her elbow.

Sssssssssssss

Mum found the keys and opened the door for me and Nan and went to switch all the lights off and I kept holding Nans arm.

Nan was two people. She was a moving slow person inside a moving very slow person. So I was walking in the smallest Guinness Book of Records steps to the door.

Nan went Ee Aa Ee Aa Ee Aa Ee every time she made a step with her legs or her sticks. When we got to the back door I looked out and guessed it was about ten normal steps to the car and that is 100 Nan steps.

Ee Aa Ee Aa Ee Aa.

I said Were nearly at the car Nan.

She kept looking at the car and laughing at me like I was mad like the car was ten miles away not ten steps away and Grandad used to say that when you get older time gets shorter and walks get longer.

Uncle Alan went past us stroking his suit and making chins and Mum shut the door and clip clopped past like a horse with two legs and Nan said to her Look at me Aa slowing you all down.

Mum said Youre not slowing us down. Were fine for time.

Nan said If you parked a bit Ee closer.

Mum said If you wait there Ill reverse the car.

Nan said I dont want to be any Ee bother pet.

Mum said Its no bother.

Mum got in the car and it went backwards and nearly knocked one of Nans silver sticks over.

Nan laughed and said to me I think theyre trying to finish us off Philip.

I kept holding the skeleton inside her skin and I didnt laugh and the car parked in front of us and I opened the door for Nan and I held her sticks and Uncle Alan said Do you need a hand back there?

And Nan said to me Some new legs would do.

Uncle Alan got out of his side of the car and helped Nan get in the car and Nan going Aa Aa Aa Watch Aa Aa and when her legs were in Uncle Alan took the metal sticks out of my hand and put them on the floor of the car in front of her.

I went round the other side and got in and sat next to her and helped her with her seat belt and she was saying I can do it pet but she couldnt.

Uncle Alan said My seats not too far back is it Philip?

I said No.

I thought he is only nice when Mum is there and then he smiled at Mum with eyes like on TV when people are in love and it made me feel sick like it was semolina in my eyes.

Mum drove to the Registry Office which is on the other side of town and the sky was grey and low down and we went past the houses that are yellow like they are ill and no one was talking. Nan was looking out at the kids and going Ssss like she was a lilo when you let the air out and we went by Players Video and J D Sports and KFC and the Chip shop and Caesars Palace. It isnt Julius Caesars Palace it is a Nightclub which is like Drama club but for people who like Night not Drama and it must be owned by someone called Caesar but not Julius. It might be owned by David Caesar or Brian Caesar or Philip Caesar.

We went past the castle wall and the castle park and the castle tramps with no teeth drinking bottles in bags on the bench. One of them saw me looking at him and his eyes stayed on me like they were trying to give me something but I didnt know what. We passed the Chinese and the Purple Door Club where Dad went once and Mum screamed at him I dont know why and Bottoms Up and the woman who shouts about God and Les Miserable walking out of Ladbrokes and we were behind a horse in a box. It was not a posh village Ra Ra horse it was a Traveller horse going left to Toney Lane where all the big gold caravans and the Travellers and the hard kids live who dont go to normal school and who can beat up anyone even Dane with their fists and big rings and we went on going past Morrisons and past all the houses and then we got there we got to the Registry Office and Newark stopped moving fast.

The Registry Office looks like nothing.

It is just a building with red bricks that you dont notice. This is on purpose so God doesnt notice and so he doesnt put lightning out of his fingers and kill the people who get married again who lied to him in the church.

Mum parked very close to the door so it wasnt far for Nan. There was a two metres tall woman at the door in a suit which was maroon and the woman said when we got out Alan and Carol?

Mum said Yes thats us.

The woman was as tall as Uncle Alan and she said We spoke on the phone. Im Angela. The Registrar.

There was a step and Nan looked at the step and a far away storm went on in her head and Angela the Registrar bent down one metre and smiled at Nan like she was a cat and she said to Nan Hello duckie do you want a wheelchair?

Nan said No pet I dont need a wheelchair.

So me and Uncle Alan helped her up the step and she went Aa Aa Aa and Mum said with crossness inside her voice but pink lips smiling at Angela the Registrar Are you sure you dont want a wheelchair Mum?

And when we got inside there was a hall and four doors and chairs in between the doors and a smelly carpet. Me and Nan sat on two chairs and no one else was there because we were early and Nan was still unflating Ssss.

Mum and Uncle Alan went to talk to Angela the Registrar and Angela the Registrar said Right if I could have your passports.

Sssssss

Mum went in her light green bag and got out two passports and Angela the Registrar said Smashing. If I could have your birth certificates.

Sssssss

Mum gave her the birth certificates and Angela the Registrar said Smashing. Right. If I could have evidence of your address E G a bill or your driving

Sssssss

Mum gave her a piece of paper and Angela the Registrar looked at it and said Smashing and then she looked at Mum and said And do you have a death certificate for your late husband?

Why are dead people late people? Dad isnt late hes early. Hes in front of everyone whos still alive because you dont start off dead you start off nothing and then you are alive and then you are dead. So it goes

Nothing

Alive

Dead

and if you are dead when you are 41 that is early not late.

Mum gave Angela the Registrar the death certificate. It was

just a bit of paper and Angela the Registrar looked at it and said Smashing.

And then people started coming.

There was Renuka who saw me and made noises because I was in a suit and Carla the Barmaid who was playing with her earrings and looking cross and moving in her suit like it had itching powder in it. She said to Ross and Gary Behave you two.

They were doing dead arms.

Ross said All right Philster?

And Gary said Is that your Nan? like Nan had no ears.

I said Yes.

Ross said Is she 100?

I said No.

Gary said Is she older than 100?

Ross said Is she 120?

I said No.

They said What older?

And I said No.

Nan said Ssssss.

Gary said 119?

And then Angela the Registrar went in one of the doors and everyone followed her like she was the Pied Piper going to the river.

The room had green stripey wallpaper and rows of chairs and a ceiling that was getting lower and lower and a carpet that was thick like grass and sinking my feet.

I was between Nan and Renuka on the second row and they were the only grown ups in the room I was taller than and I was feeling weird like my brain was going too fast and I wished Id had my tablet.

Angela the Registrar nodded her high head and made wide eyes at a man at the end of the room and said Derek music and some Derek music came on.

Then she said Derek and the music stopped.

Angela the Registrar looked at Uncle Alan and Mum standing there and Renuka came up in a whisper saying Doesnt your Mum look beautiful Philip?

I looked at Mums bare back over her dress and her bare neck and I said Yes.

She said I bet youre proud.

I said nothing.

And Angela the Registrar pressed her hands together and said Id like to start by welcoming you all to

He was there standing behind. Dads Ghost.

He said You have to stop this Philip.

Angela the Registrar said If any persons present know of any lawful impediment why Alan and Carol may not be joined together in matrimony please speak now.

Dads Ghost said Say something Philip. Tell them about Uncle Alan. Tell them the truth Philip. The truth.

Angela the Registrar looked at Uncle Alan and said If you can say after me.

He said after her I do solemnly declare that I know not of any lawful impediment why I Alan Peter Noble may not be joined in matrimony to Carol Suzanne Noble.

And then Mum said it and put more Nobles in the room.

I do Noble why I Noble know not Noble may not Noble in Noble to Noble Noble Noble.

Dads Ghost was screaming No! No! No!

And the ceiling was getting low low low and the carpet was growing grow grow grow and I looked behind and saw all the other faces looking at Uncle Alan and Mums backs and then it happened the big blue giant and the little green Mum turned to each other and the words came out of him into Mums eyes.

I call upon these persons here present to witness that I Alan Peter Noble do take thee Carol Suzanne Noble to be my lawful wedded wife and Nan went Ssssss and Renuka touched her eye and went Awwwww and Dads Ghost looked at Mum and said Dont do it dont say it dont say it I still love you please and Mum smiling up into Uncle Alans face I call upon these persons here present Dont do it witness that I Carol Suzanne Noble Awwwww do take thee Alan I still Peter love you No to be my lawful wedded husband Ssssssssssssssssssssssssssssssssssssssssssssssss

I am dizzy and I blink and I am in the car park holding Nans elbow and Uncle Alan in front lifting Mum up and taking her in the door like the Romans did and Mum laughing and Uncle Alan laughing and Nan looking at me with her eyes like little milk plates for a cat to drink and her mouth with no lips saying It wont Aa last son it wont last.

The Garage

Dads Ghost said They get worse. The Terrors. They get much worse.

I said I know. Im going to do it today. Im going to let you Rest In Peace.

I put the last of my weapons the **MAGNESIUM GRANULES** in my bag and I waited for Dads Ghost to fade into the air and then I went to school.

I didnt want to go out at the breaks so I stayed in the school library and read Horrible Histories and after school I didnt go home straight away I walked through the quiet roads and past all the windows and some had Christmas trees and Angels in them and then I got to a shop which was called LONDIS.

It was a shop I never went to so no one would see me and I said Can I have a box of matches?

And the woman was sitting on a chair and reading Heat which is the magazine Renuka always takes for Mum. The woman was pale like a dead Guppy and I wondered if you cut her if she would bleed white blood.

She looked up from the magazine like she didnt have the strength to get the matches. Like the magazine was a colour magnet sucking out her colour. She said Bonfire Night was weeks ago.

I said I know.

She said Youre too young to smoke.

I said I dont want cigarettes. Just matches.

She got off her chair and turned round and got the matches like it was the biggest job in the world and I paid with my dinner money.

The matches were called Vestas.

Vesta is the Roman god of fire and the Vestal Virgins kept a flame going for ever in a temple which was round.

I put the matches in my pocket and the pale woman went back inside her magazine and I went outside and walked to the Garage.

It was nearly dark and the day shadows were nearly rubbed out by the night but there were some shadows from the street lamp that flickered like a ghost.

The Garage was on its own. There were no shops or anything near it. Only the Tech. But not the main entrance to the Tech just the fence. The Garage was near the middle of town but not on a main street. It was off the corner of a street like an L like it was hiding.

The L street had no name because there was no sign but it was near Friary Road where the Tech is and where the park is where people walk dogs.

And the Garage had two doors there was a big door that was like a big wooden wall and there was a door inside the door that was a normal door and the doors were both closed so it was all wooden planks going down but the lines round the little door were light so there was someone in.

I got the Magnesium out of my bag and I put the granules in a line on the ground by the door and they were bright even though it was getting darker and darker.

I felt in my pocket for the matches and I got them out. I tried to look through the crack in the door to see inside the Garage because I didnt want to kill any customers or Sleepy Eye Terry I just wanted to kill Uncle Alan.

I saw a shadow go past but I couldnt tell if it was Uncle Alans shadow. And then I heard Dads Ghost behind me.

He knew what I was thinking and he said Its only him Philip. Its only Uncle Alan. Hes the only one there. All the customers are gone. Thats why the doors are shut.

I looked round and Dads Ghost was standing in front of the wire fence of the Tech and he said Theres no one else.

His voice said Do it Philip.

Do it.

Do it.

Do it.

Light the match.

Light it Philip.

Go on.

Light it.

The Land of Nod

There were 200 tongues coming from mouths under the ground licking the wood and I looked at it for a minute and my face was hot and I couldnt see Dads Ghost but he said Run.

I said Bye Dad. I love you.

He said Run!

I heard something inside the Garage. A screaming sound. And I thought Its him! Its him!

And I ran away from the fire and I kept running and I heard a noise like a bang and then a noise like a sucking noise like the Garage was trying to breathe and I turned and saw fire come out of the door in a circle.

I kept running past the Tech. The bikes locked to the fence looked weird in the dark. They looked like lots of big glasses all looking at me. And when I got to the main road I stopped running and I looked to see Dads Ghost but he wasnt anywhere. He was in the Garage watching Uncle Alan die in the flames and then Dads Ghost was going to Rest In Peace for ever.

I walked down the main road and there was no one because it was freezing and I went past the tennis courts and through the park so no cars saw me and I saw the smoke. It was black clouds going up to rub out the stars.

I thought Oh no what if the fire doesnt stop? What if it is like Rome in the year 64 AD which kept on burning? Or the Great Fire of London in the year 1666 AD? What if I have started the Great Fire of Newark? Or the Great Fire of England and the whole of the country burns and everyone has to live on the island in the water in Rufford Park where me and Mum and Dad went when I was little.

I saw Les Miserable on Bridge Street and he was walking with a woman and when he saw me he stopped holding the womans hands and he saw me looking at him and he made clouds out of his mouth and said All right Phil lad?

I said Yes.

I kept walking and then I heard a fire engine go neenar-neenar and I ran to the Pub and went in the back way and went upstairs and I heard Mums feet go out of the Pub to the hall and Mums voice go upstairs Philip? Philip? Philip?

I said Yes.

Mum climbed the stairs and she said Where the HELL have you been?

I said Out. I went out.

The flames crackled him like pork and he screamed and screamed and it was too late.

Mum said What do you mean out? Out where?

I said Just out.

The hoses sprayed water all over and it rained on the Garage but the fire and the smoke didnt stop until Uncle Alan was a ghost and Dad could tell him what happened.

I had killed Uncle Alan and I wanted to see Dads Ghost because Dads Ghost was the only person who knew I had killed him. But Dads Ghost was gone and out of the Terrors and in Heaven or in Nothing.

I lay on my bed and I waited for the phone to ring or for Mum to get worried but Mum wasnt getting worried and I thought of Les Miserable and the woman I saw and what if they told the police they saw me. I was thinking about Uncle Alan and all the worry was like electric inside my body and all my veins were metal wires that were CONDUCTING the electric.

I had killed him and crackled him and now his life was inside me. I had taken it and one body is not made for two lives and it was too much electric in my wires so I couldnt stay lying down. I went into the hallway and said Mum in a shout.

I said Mum Mum.

And she came out of the bar to the bottom of the stairs and she said Sssh.

I said Why?

She said Youll wake Alan.

I said What?

She said Youll wake Alan.

I said What?

She said Youll wake Alan.

I walked downstairs and I said Uncle Alans in the Garage. Hes in the Garage.

Mum said He came home this afternoon with a headache. Hes been in the Land of Nod ever since.

Mum said Are you all right Philip? You look like youve seen a

I ran up the stairs faster than her question and I went into Mum and Dads bedroom and he was there on the bed lying down with his big stomach like a hill and snoring like a pig not crackled like one.

I thought he might be a ghost and Mum didnt know he was a ghost. But he wasnt see through and ghosts dont sleep or bend the bed and I thought Oh no.

I remembered the sound in the Garage. The screaming sound. It came back in my ears Aaaaaaaa and my face went hot like I was still in front of the fire and I thought Oh no. Oh no. Oh no. Oh no.

I looked round the room at the city of pots and tubs and tans and the mirror and Uncle Alan inside the mirror still in the Land of Nod. I wanted Dads Ghost but he wasnt there and I went out of the room and downstairs and into the Pub and all the faces were laughing. Big Vic and Carla and Mum. They looked like Devils. Big Vic said I swear down its the fucking truth.

They all laughed again and then Carla saw me and said All right Philip love?

And Mum turned and said You didnt wake Alan up did you?

And Big Vic looked at me like I was a Big Money question on the Millionaire Machine that he couldnt work out and that was when the phone went ring ring.

But it was the Pub phone and that phone goes more like a sheep Baa baa Baa baa.

Mum went out into the hallway still laughing and she picked it up and said Hello?

I watched her face as her laugh got ill and died.

There was nothing in the world just Mums voice and Mums words.

Yes.

Yes?

What kind of accident?

No.

Oh God.

No.
Are you sure?
At the?
No.
Was anyone?
No hes here now. Hes upstairs.
I cant believe it.
Yes of course.
What right now?
Here at the Pub?
Just Alan or both of us?
Yes.
Yes I will.
Yes.
Bye.
Bye.

The questions had jaws like crocodiles doing big yawns and snapping in my head.

Who was the Scream? Who was it? Was it Sleepy Eye Terry? Was it the Other Man who smashed the Pub? Was it a customer? Was it in my mind? It was in my mind yes it was in my mind yes yes it was in my mind.

But then Mum was off the phone and then there was the answer and it gobbled me up in one bite.

Mr Fairview is dead

The Voices Out of the Wall

The policeman with his plate face looked at the rings on Mums Wedding finger and asked her And where was your son at this time?

And Mum looked at me and Uncle Alan looked at Mum.

Mum said He was here. He came back from school at four. He was upstairs in his room. While Alan was asleep.

The policeman wrote this down and he didnt know it was a lie and Uncle Alan didnt know it was a lie but it was a lie and I looked at Mum and she looked at me like she knew what Id done.

I said Can I go to bed?

Mum said Yes.

The policeman with the empty plate face just looked at me and I went upstairs and into my room and Dads Ghost wasnt there.

And I just waited and I heard the police go and I heard

Mum and Uncle Alan go upstairs and I heard them talking about Mr Fairview in the next room.

Uncle Alan said What the Hell was he doing there? Hes never at the Garage.

Mum said Come on. Try not to think about that.

Uncle Alan said It makes no sense.

Mum said These things never do.

Uncle Alan said What the Hell was he doing there?

Mum said God knows.

Uncle Alan said It makes no sense.

I put the duvet over my head and the voices went away but other things started so I put my head over the duvet and heard Mum say Your whisky.

Uncle Alan said Thanks.

Mum said Do you think it was our son?

I sat up in bed like when I have the insect dream and my heart was beating like mad beatbeatbeat and then Uncle Alan said Arson?

Mum said Yes so my heart started to slow down.

Uncle Alan said Who knows? Who the Hell knows?

Mum said You dont think

Uncle Alan said What?

Mum said You dont think he did it on purpose?

Uncle Alan said Done himself in?

There was quiet and then there was Uncle Alan saying No I cant see why hed do that. Hes got two kids. And hes in the God Squad. Hes hardly going to miss his chance of Heaven. And hardly the way to go is it. I mean if you were choosing.

Mum said But he lost his wife didnt he?

Uncle Alan said A few years back that was.

Mum said I still cant believe it.

Uncle Alan said Mind you hes been acting a bit weird lately. Asking for the books. I bet he was having a snoop about the place.

Mum said Those poor kids.

Uncle Alan said Itll be a lot you know.

Mum said What will?

Uncle Alan said The pay out.

They started talking quieter after that.

I couldnt hear the words just the voices that got mixed up with the noises of the trains and the lorries and the wind and the barking dogs and all the noises the town makes to keep bad people awake all night.

This Bastard Town

I was outside and running out of the car park and away from town. I ran past the level crossing and past all the Saturday Ra Ras going into the Waitrose car park.

I passed the sign that said

You are now leaving historic Newark-on-Trent

but someone had done a line of paint over **historic Newark-on-Trent** and put THIS BASTARD TOWN above it.

I kept going until there were no houses just the fields that are bright yellow in summer but are brown in December and the pavement got thinner and thinner until it wasnt a pavement and I kept running on the side of the road and I had pains in my side but I kept going and the cars were going faster now and beeping beeep! but I didnt care about the cars I didnt care.

After a bit I had to walk because the pain was like a knife and my tongue was stinging but it was a fast walk with bits of running slow as well. It felt weird walking on the main road out of town like I was getting less real on every step away like I might turn into nothing.

I kept going and looking behind until the church was small and I was at the Sugar Factory and the Sugar Factory was halfway to Kelham.

Beep!

Beeep!

Beeeep!

The Sugar Factory has a weird smell. It is not like sugar and it gets in your mouth and makes you feel sick.

After a bit the pylons started and I looked at them and they were giant robots ruling the land and stopping humans get too tall with their weapons which were deadly wires swooping in the sky.

Twenty minutes later I got to the bridge past all the trees and it was the first time I had seen it since Dad died apart from on East Midlands Today.

The road was quieter now and there was a thin pavement again and the sky was still light but it was starting to get dark and I looked at the bridge from across the road.

Dads car crashed right through the middle bit. You could see where they had mended the bridge because the new bricks looked too new and the old bricks looked too old and the cement in between all the new bricks was too white.

There were grey stones on the very top of the bricks but the new grey stones were lighter grey because time makes everything go darker.

I looked on the road to see if I could see any black skid marks but there wasnt anything just the bits of the road that had been made more shiny by car tyres and they were all going in straight lines. They were not going into the bridge because only one car crashed into the bridge and that was Dads car.

A motorbike went past and it roared like a lion and when it went past it meowed like a cat and after it had gone I crossed over the road.

When I got there I bent down and I touched the old bricks and then I touched the new bricks and they felt different. I thought of Dad in the car on his own and I rubbed the new bricks like they were a cut you could make better.

The crash happened in my head. The tyres made a scream and the bricks crashed and Dads face was all scared and I didnt know if the brakes were working or if they had broken but I didnt care because he wasnt going to come back and speak to me or go in the snow with me.

Even if his ghost came back it wasnt the same and I didnt want his ghost any more. I wanted him. I wanted everything to be normal the way it was. I didnt know why things couldnt stay the same way for ever and if they couldnt stay the same why did you have to have the things in the first place? Why cant you just be a tree or a brick and not know anything?

I used to think Dad was the best Dad in the world but I dont know if he was. He screamed sometimes and he put me under the stairs in the dark cupboard when he was mad with me when I broke the window.

Dads are just men who have babies but I know he loved me because I felt it go out of me when he crashed. It was like air or blood or bones or something that made me me and it wasnt there any more and I had only half of it now and I didnt know if that was enough.

And I thought about Mr Fairview and I wondered if Leah and Dane felt it go out of them and it didnt matter that it was

an accident just like it didnt matter if Dads crash was an accident because it still happened and its what happens that matters
not why.

At the bottom of the bridge wall there were weeds under the
old bricks but not under the new ones. The new bricks didnt
have any holes and no room for weeds. But one day the weeds
will find a way into the new bricks because weeds can grow anywhere Dad told me.

And I touched the bricks one more time and I started walking home.

Spitting to the Grass

I got back into town on London Road and I heard a voice and it was someone shouting Oi Philster. I turned and it was Ross and Gary and they were sitting on a bench near the big grass triangle and they were in massive Nike trainers and they said Come here like they couldnt move. Like the trainers were big heavy weights that stuck them to the ground.

I went over even though I didnt want to. I didnt want to do anything ever again because things go wrong when you do things. But they had the remote control for me and I said What?

Ross said How far can you spit?

I said Dont know.

Gary said Could you get the grass from here?

I said Dont know.

Ross said Try.

Gary said But youve got to sit down on the bench.

Ross said Yeah try from the bench.

I sat down on the bench and I was still on remote control

and I saw all the spit circles on the path. Some were still white and foamy and some were dark and nearly dry. Ross did a spit and it nearly got the grass and Gary did one and it got even closer and then they looked at me. I tried to spit but I was thinking about Leah and I got nowhere near where their spit landed. They laughed but then stopped quickly and Gary said It was well mad about the fire.

I said Yeah.

Ross said It must be cool to set things on fire. I mean big things like a Garage.

He looked at me for a long time.

I said I suppose.

Gary said in a light heavy voice Did you do it Philster? Was it you?

I said No too quick and then tried to laugh but it came out weird like the laugh had been smashed with a hammer and all the pieces were put back together wrong and then I said Course not. Course I didnt.

Ross said We wont grass you up or owt.

Gary said I mean it was just cool thats all.

I was thinking of Leah again and I said I didnt I didnt I didnt do it.

Ross said Chill. Its all right. We was only asking.

Gary said Yeah only asking chav.

I said Yeah I know.

Ross said You like our trainers?

I didnt care about their trainers but I said Yeah.

Gary said Air Hercules.

Ross said We got them as a present.

Gary hit Rosss arm when he said that like it was a secret.

I said Oh.

And then they started spitting again trying to reach the grass but I didnt try this time. I just sat there watching the spit circles bubble out and then I got up and said See you later.

They said See you Philster.

See you mate.

But it didnt sound right this time like the word mate was an insect that went in my ears and stayed in my head.

When I got back to the Pub I went past the bins and there were bags by the bins and two said JD Sport and I saw through the bags and there were boxes with the Nike sign on them.

I checked to see if anyone was watching and there was no one only ghosts I couldnt see so I got the box out and I looked inside and I saw the sticker and it said Nike Air Hercules and there was a piece of blue paper in the bag and it said Nike Air Hercules x 2 and it had Uncle Alans writing on it and I knew hed bought them to get Ross and Gary to spy on me. And I heard Gary again in my head Did you do it Philster? Was it you?

I knew from then that there was no one in the whole world who is who you think they are. You cant trust anyone. Not the dead or the living. They all lie all the time and hide things you cant see but you can smell it if you know how and when you do it is stronger than a Stink Bomb. I went inside and I went to my room and closed my eyes and I had a feeling like another bad thing was going to happen.

Ghost Words

Dads Ghost came in the night and his excuses fell into my head
one by one.
    It was a mistake Philip it was a mistake
    I was flickering out
    It was hard to see
    I couldnt see properly Philip
    He looked like Uncle Alan son
    He looked like Uncle Alan
    Do you think I wanted this to happen?
    Do you think thats what I wanted?
    I wanted it to be Uncle Alan
    It had to be Uncle Alan
    If you had acted sooner
    If you hadnt waited
    Why didnt you?
    Why didnt you do something before?
    Youve been a slow coach Philip

A slow coach
Im sorry son but you have
No
Im sorry I didnt mean
Philip I shouldnt have said
Philip I
Philip
Philip son
Phil
Ph
And I said Go away. Just go away.

Dead and Gone Dead and Gone

I had to tell Leah and Dane the Truth.

I had to tell them before Mr Fairviews Ghost told them so I went and asked Mum. She was doing her workout with her hands and knees on the floor and lifting out one knee at a time like a dog going for a wee.

I said Can I go out for one hour? Can I go to the library?

The library wasnt open on Sundays but Mum didnt know so it was a good excuse.

Bobby with the muscles on the DVD said You should be really feeling it by now.

Mum kept lifting her knee and she looked at me and said Ill drive you round. After my workout.

Bobby said Really burn those glutes. Feel it burning. Burning down the house.

I said Can I go on my own?

She said OK. Yes. But an hour thats all. Not like yesterday.

I didnt care if Dane and Leah told the police on me but I was a bit scared that Dane was going to kill me because then I might get the Terrors.

But I was thinking that the Terrors might just be another lie and maybe Dads Ghost wasnt Dads Ghost at all it might just be the Devil trying to get me to do bad things like kill Mr Fairview because he liked God not the Devil.

Danes skin head came to me in the fuzzy glass and he opened the door. I was scared he was going to kill me right then but he looked at me like a stranger or like I was just space or the water in a tank and I said Hi.

The Hi sounded stupid the way things always sound stupid when people die and I wanted to tell him It was me I killed him but I didnt.

He didnt say Hi back but he let me in.

There was no one in the house except Leah and Dane. I thought maybe they were going to live together now on their own with no grown ups.

I went upstairs and pushed open Leahs door and she was there sitting on the bed in her coat with the fur round the hood that made her look like an animal. An animal that might climb trees. I said Leah?

But the word was invisible to her ears.

Leah?

Leah its me.

Philip.

I sat next to her on the bed and saw her face in the reflection of the window. It was see through like a ghost and it wasnt crying it was not anything and I looked round at the posters all smiling like they didnt care and I said Leah Im sorry.

She was digging her right thumbnail into her left hand making a little blood smile and she said in a slow voice quiet like air nearly singing Dead and gone dead and gone.

There was a letter by the window and there were two tickets in a blue holder that said Air New Zealand and I said Are they from your aunt? Are you going to live in New Zealand?

Her head fell a bit on her left side and her eyes went wider in the window and she kept on saying it Dead and gone dead and gone dead and gone dead and gone dead and gone.

I said Leah. Leah?

And I saw her nail digging deeper in her hand and I tried to look at her face but it was just her hood so I looked in the window and I jumped because there was someone else next to her in the glass with a red face like the Devil and he had his arm round her and he said If it isnt little Philip?

Mr Fairview Makes Me
Tell the Truth

I got off the bed very quick and I looked and he was there next to Leah. His burnt face was looking at me behind her hood and his burnt hand was on her shoulder. It was Mr Fairview in black clothes like coal with holes in them and redness coming through the holes and Leah couldnt see him or hear him. She was digging her nail and singing a pop song in a whisper

Tomorrow is Saint Valentines Day

And I dont expect no flowers

The best I can hope is to stay like this

Counting down the hours

Mr Fairview stood up off the bed and he had no hair on his head and no eyebrows. He just had twisty scars all over like screwed up paper and he came close to me and he said He cant handle the Terrors little Philip.

I said Please.

Leah kept on singing and Mr Fairview said with his finger on his invisible lips Sssh. Sssh. Can you hear that Philip? Can you hear his screams? He is screaming your name Philip but you cant hear him. Can you hear him Philip?

I shook my head.

Mr Fairview said There is no peace unto the wicked. No peace. Are you wicked Philip? Have you done a wicked thing? I think you must have Philip. I think that is why I am here. Have you been wicked?

I shook my head.

Mr Fairview went quiet and I could see the black bone in his jaw and his skin flapping and he said Even the ghosts dont want him now Philip.

I said Please leave me alone.

Mr Fairview said clubs have rules.

I said Please.

Mr Fairview said I told them the truth Philip.

I scrunched my eyes shut but I could still hear his voice.

I opened my eyes and looked at Leah and she was in her hood and making mumble sounds and Mr Fairview looked at her and said My Lambkin.

Then he looked at me and said Tell the truth Philip.

He kept on saying it over and over and over Tell the truth tell the truth tell the truth tell the truth.

And his words pushed me back into the wardrobe and then I ran out of the room and down the stairs and past the words on the wall in the frame Ye shall know the truth and the truth shall make you free and I got to the back door and Dane was outside smoking.

Mr Fairview flickered on next to him and screamed from the Terrors and then he said You must tell him Philip. You must get it out of your system Philip. Or I will be here for ever Philip. I will follow you wherever you go.

I said Dane.

He looked at me and he sucked the cigarette inside him.

I said Dane again.

A What? came out of a smoke cloud.

I looked at his big hand as he sucked the cigarette with wide fingers and nearly no nails.

I said I know who started the fire.

Dane looked at me like Id pushed him and he said What?

I said I know who started the fire.

He did a smoke circle out his mouth and blew more smoke and broke it.

Dane said Philip just leave it.

Dane didnt understand so I said I cant.

I looked out and saw the backs of the other houses on the street behind and there were no lights in any of the windows so no one was there and no one was going to see Dane kill me.

He said What you fucking on about?

He flicked the cigarette on the ground and it rolled on the concrete and into a puddle and went out.

He got something out of his pocket something black and pulled metal out of it like a mirror but it wasnt a mirror it was a knife. He started scraping out the cement in the wall and making a cloud of dust.

Mr Fairviews Ghost looked at me and said Say it.

I said I did it.

Dane said What?

I said The fire.

He said What you talking about?

A dog started barking in one of the other backyards and the bark turned into a cry.

Mr Fairview said Say it again.

I said I did the fire. I started the fire at the Garage.

The words were inside Danes brain now getting bigger I

STARTED THE FIRE AT THE GARAGE and pushing out his eyes.

He said with a quiet voice and a loud face You what?

I said I started the fire.

His hand that wasnt holding the knife was on my face and squeezing my cheeks and pulling my head up out of my body.

I said Im sorry. It was an accident. I meant to kill Uncle Alan.

He couldnt hear my words properly because I couldnt move my mouth because his hand was squeezing my cheeks.

Mr Fairviews Ghost was in Danes ear now and saying Do it son. Kill him. Get my Revenge. Let me rest.

Dane pushed the back of my head against the brick wall by the kitchen window and it hurt and then I felt cold metal on my neck and I thought in 20 seconds I will be DEAD. He will chop off my head and stick it in a jar like the Druids did when the Romans came to England.

He said Shut up shut up shut up.

I said Im sorry. I went to the Garage. I had some Magnesium. I set it on fire to kill my uncle.

He said Why you fucking saying that?

I said Im sorry.

He said What the fucks up with you?

I said Im sorry.

He said WHAT THE FUCKS UP WITH YOU?

I said Im sorry Dane Im sorry. I didnt know your dad was in there.

Mr Fairview said to Dane Let me rest. Let me rest.

The knife was tickling my neck and I closed my eyes and I waited for it to go in and splurt blood all over Danes face and over his earring in his eyebrow. I wondered how long it would take for my brain to die and I hoped hed do it properly not how

Emperor Nero did it when he wanted to kill himself and had to get his soldiers to help him because he hadnt pushed the knife right in.

I thought KILL ME QUICK KILL ME QUICK KILL ME QUICK but then I thought of the Terrors and of Mum and I thought I dont want to die.

And my eyes were open now and I saw the sky that was clear with all the stars. Some of them were dead and some of them were alive but you couldnt tell because the light was still shining.

Mr Fairview said Do it son. Press the knife.

And Dane said to himself Do it! Fucking do it! Do it! Fucking do it! Cunt! Do it!

And I thought that was it that was the full stop but it wasnt because he threw the knife down and he roared like he was an animal. I didnt know why he threw down the knife. I didnt know if it was because of Leah or New Zealand or his dad.

He turned and I looked at his back and he said in the quietest voice in the world Dont come round again or Ill kill you Philip. If you tell Leah Ill kill you. Ill kill you. I fucking swear.

And he didnt turn round and I went to the gate and I opened it and I started walking and Mr Fairview stayed with Dane and didnt follow.

Someone to See Me

It was December the 6th and that meant there was only four days to go before Dads Ghost had to have the Terrors for ever.

And I didnt know what to do because I didnt know what was true and what was not true. I used to think things go wrong because you are a wimp and wait too long and dont do things but I knew now that things go wrong when you do things and they are the wrong things. And even if they are the right things they still go wrong in the end because doing one thing is impossible because you do one thing and another thing always happens and another thing and another thing and another thing and another thing and another thing and even more things.

It was the weekend and Sleepy Eye Terry had been in the Living Room all morning talking to Uncle Alan and Mum about Mr Fairviews funeral which they went to on the day before. And then Uncle Alan and Sleepy Eye Terry went downstairs and out and so I dared to go in the Living Room and see Mum.

I said Wheres Uncle Alan?

She was putting the washing in the washing machine and she said Hes gone fishing. I told him to. He needs to take his mind off You Know.

She didnt look at me in the eyes. She hadnt looked at me in the eyes since she told the lie to the policeman.

I thought about helping Mum with the washing but I didnt I just went back into my room and did nothing for two hours. I just stared at the ceiling and pretended to take my pill when Mum asked me.

I thought about telling Dads Ghost to go away and now I wished I hadnt because if Mr Fairview was right Dads Ghost was not allowed in the Dead Fathers Club and so he had no one.

I heard Mums voice and she said Yes yes. He is. Ill just get him.

And then she called up the stairs Philip? Philip love? Theres someone to see you.

And I went downstairs and Mum wasnt there. It was just the door open and Dane was standing there with his skin head growing out his eyebrow growing scabs and I thought He has changed his mind and he is going to knife me.

I got to the door and waited for him to knife me but he didnt have a knife. He just said Shes gone.

I said What?

His eyes looked like they had been taken out and put back in.

He said Have you seen her? Has she been round here?

My heart fell like a pebble inside me and I wished he was going to kill me and I said No.

I saw Leah in my head. I saw her trying to save me from the boys and her red and brown hair blowing to me.

I said Shes not been here.

His eyes were jerking all over and he said to himself Ive got to look for her Ive got to keep looking keep looking keep look-ing. And his eyes stopped jerking and saw a brick a half brick on the ground in the car park and he picked it up and he went over to Carlas little white car and he smashed the window and he got in and sat down on the glass and he bent down so I couldnt see him and was ten seconds and then the car did a cough and started and he shut the door of the car and zoomed out the car park and the tyres cried when he skidded off like they were scared.

The Paper Bird

I said into the air Dad.

I said Dad come back.

I said Dad Dad. Come back. I need you.

I said Dad please. I need to find Leah. Shes in trouble. Shes gone missing.

I went out to the Bottle Banks but I still couldnt see Dads Ghost and I said Can anyone help me? Ray? Ray Goodwin? I need to find Mr Fairviews daughter. She is called Leah. Can anyone help? Mr Fairview? Are you there?

I heard a voice behind me and at first I thought it was one of the ghosts and the voice said All right Philip?

And the voice was laughing and I turned round and it was Big Vic and he was jingling his car keys jingle jingle and he was with Les Miserable and Les Miserable didnt say anything he just looked down and zipped up his jacket which was weird because they were going to go into the Pub and Big Vic said Talking to the Bottle Banks?

He was still laughing and they looked weird standing there thin Les and fat Vic side by side like a number 10 and I didnt say anything and my quietness stopped Vics laughing. Then the wind started and Les Miserable didnt want to speak to me because I had seen him with the woman and he had seen me near the fire and he said to Vic with his not moving mouth Come on its getting raw.

His head nodded backwards to the Pub like his hair was iron filings and the Pub was a magnet and they turned round and the wind pushed them to the Pub and I heard Big Vic and he said Hes a fucking fruit and nut that kid.

I saw a piece of paper on the ground. It was the Newark Advertiser and it was the front page and the back page. The front page had a picture of the Garage all black from the fire and the word **TRAGEDY** and then the wind unfolded the paper and the words were **GARAGE FIRE TRAGEDY**. The paper flew into the air like it was a bird with wings.

I followed it out of the car park and onto the road.

I kept on following the paper and it went down Castlegate and then it went down another road and then it stopped for a minute and I thought that was weird because Leah wasnt there but then it started moving and people were looking at me strange but I didnt care. I kept following the paper and it went down a passage and out and I thought Oh no because I knew where we were. We were at the river.

The ground was concrete and then it was grass and then longer grass and there was a path very thin and I ran because the paper was taking off now and going quickly and I looked back for one second and the buildings were going it was just grass now and the wind whispered We are near.

I looked forward and kept running following the paper and it was high and hard to see because of the bright clouds then I heard a noise like a toilet flush but louder and not going away. I knew what it was. It was the weir. And the wind was saying we are near weir near.

I shouted LEAH! And there was nothing. Just the weir getting louder and the paper getting closer.

LEAH!

LEAH!

LEAH!

And then the paper started to come down from the sky and when it came down I stopped running and followed it with my eyes and then I saw her and she was standing high on the bridge with her arms out like Jesus.

She was standing on the wall of the bridge not on the bit you walk and the water was below her and the weir was foam like white clouds like a waterfall and it was far down like a swimming pool off a diving board but not like a swimming pool because you die if you go in the weir everyone knows.

She had a top on with short sleeves like it was summer and not the coldest day in the world.

LEAH!

LEAH!

Her red and brown hair was blowing all wild like it was alive and didnt want to die with the rest of her.

LEAH!

LEAH!

She couldnt hear me because the water was so loud it was like there was nothing else just the water so I ran closer shouting and she turned and saw me and turned back and looked down at the water and I was very scared she was going to jump in the water and the newspaper wrapped round her legs and then up and away into nowhere.

Standing on the Bridge

I said DONT.

I said DONT LEAH DONT. COME DOWN. ITS MY FAULT. DONT.

I was shouting because of the weir noise and Leah put her arms down and her arms were pink like sausages because of the cold and she had words on them not in blue pen in red blood DEAD + GONE.

She turned and looked down at me and she saw me but she didnt say anything and her face looked empty like the shops near Nans with wood in the windows and then she looked back down at the water and I got closer to her and I said LEAH GET DOWN!

My words got drowned.

I looked down the path to see if anyone was coming and there he was Dads Ghost. He was standing there in his red T shirt but his arms werent cold and he said Be careful Philip. You cant change whats happened.

He didnt care about Leah and that made me mad so I said IT WAS YOU IT WAS YOUR FAULT YOU DID IT YOU KILLED HIM IT WAS YOU.

Leah turned round because I was louder now and she could hear.

I was speaking to Dads Ghost but Leah didnt know I was speaking to Dads Ghost because she couldnt see Dads Ghost because she had her back to the path and she couldnt see ghosts.

I turned and said LEAH NO!

But it was too late and she was falling forward her body all straight like a door and I ran to the wall and saw her drop down into the water and land with a little white splash.

I climbed onto the bridge wall and the wind got angry and Dads Ghost said No.

I could see two fishermen miles away in the distance and I shouted HELP! HELP!

But they couldnt hear me.

I looked down at Leahs white splash and I looked at the weir.

I was meant to not go into the water. That is what I was meant to do. Just do nothing. And Leah would die and I wouldnt die so I could stay alive and kill Uncle Alan like Dads Ghost said.

That is what the stars said and everything said but I had a strange feeling like when you are dreaming and first you are watching your dream and you have no control of your dream but then when you are still sleeping you think I AM DREAM-ING and as soon as you think that you start to change the dream the way you want to like you can turn the insects on your plate into raisins again.

And when I was standing on the wall on the bridge I thought life is not like a film or a Christmas play or a TV with only one channel. There are more channels. You can change the story and turn over or do something different it is up to you.

And Dads Ghost was saying Philip no! Dont jump! Philip! Dont jump!

And my body was saying Philip no! Dont jump! Philip! Dont jump! But there is a different voice that is louder than the voice of ghosts and the voice of bodies and that voice was the voice I heard when I put my foot onto the air and fell into the water.

In the River

When I fell it was weird.

It was like my body was moving faster than me and I was still on the bridge looking at the water. My body kept falling through all the universe and then hit the water and I was back inside of my body.

I went down into the black water down down and it was burning cold and it was pulling me to the weir and I kicked my legs and it was not like in the swimming pool in pyjamas because the water was strong like it was angry with me.

Then I thought of Leah and that made me stronger and I got into air and I saw the back of her head all wet and shiny like a football going closer to the weir. I started swimming but the cold was freezing my arms and hurting them and slowing them but I kept seeing Leahs head go under the water and that is what kept me going.

LEAH!

LEAH!

She turned round in the water and she didnt look scared. She didnt look anything. I thought she might be dead already but she wasnt and the water kept on trying to get in my mouth and up my nose and pull me down but I kept on swimming closer to Leah and closer to the weir and the water and I kicked my shoes off in the water because they were heavy.

She was near where the black water meets the white water and as soon as she got into the white water she was going to go under it so I had to grab her.

I got hold of her and I said KICK YOUR LEGS but it was really kick your legs because of the weir noise.

LEAH LEAH KICK YOUR LEGS

And then I tried to shout Help! to the fishermen but they couldnt hear and that was when we got to the white water that was going to make us die.

In the White Water

Her eyes know what she has done now and water jumps into her mouth and turns into a cough and I lose her and she goes under and I cant see her but my arm goes after her and gets her and I pull her up and she is back in the world and she gasps the air in and I am holding her arm her wrist and we are trying to swim away from the white and the noise but I cant even do one press up and I am not Spiderman and the water is pulling all of nature is pulling and we go backwards into the foam and the water punches us all over and we go down fast on our backs down the weir like nothing like bits of wood and I cant see and I cant hear and the water pulls Leahs coat from the other side like a tug of war and the water wins.

And the water is everywhere it is in my eyes and in my nose and in my ears and in my mouth and I am caught under the waterfall and it is raining air and I look for Leah but I cant see her and a fish touches my face and flies off and I am swimming like a frog upside down with the water still pushing me and I can feel the river bed I can feel its slime sticking to me and hugging me and wanting me to stay there but there is air in me so I float up off the slime and twist and swim in the blackness and keep swimming up keep swimming but the world is miles away and I am losing air in pebbles out of my mouth cant breathe cant breathe and the river is squeezing the air out like toothpaste squeezing hard Where is Leah? Where is she? it is at my throat the panic and I need to breathe in I am not a fish no gills my body is a machine a breathing air machine in and out and in and out and it needs to breathe in now it needs to breathe in something something on my shoulder something a hand pulling up I cant wait I cant wait my body cant breathe in breathe in now breathe

newark trout

come and say hello to mr fairview
        with your arms and legs off the floor you can feel
        like you are flying

    after years spent in warm sunshine

                under normal circumstances
                                straight out of the trent
we would have no choice but to take philip out of

the unknown world
        to go deep underground and work in the dark

in the name of god

in the name of

in the name of god

Lying on the Mud

Philip?

    Philip lad.

    Philip can you hear me?

    Philip.

    Philip?

    Philip lad open your eyes.

    Philip try and open your eyes.

    Philip?

    Philip?

    My eyes hatch open and he is there the voice is there.

    He is blocking out the sky. It is Uncle Alan and he is looking very worried and he says Philip can you hear me? If you can hear me say Yes. If you can hear me son say Yes.

    I say Yes.

    He stands up seven miles tall and he moves away and I turn my head which is as heavy as the world and I follow his back and I see Leah on the ground on the mud lying down dead with a man doing Save a Life on her mouth and then on her heart with his hands and Uncle Alan is talking to the man pointing to the water.

Uncle Alan screams IVE GOT TO GET HIM.

And the man I can see his face now his half closed eye it is Sleepy Eye Terry and he is still pushing on Leahs heart and he says WHO?

THERES SOMEONE ELSE IN THE WATER.

Terry looks at the water THERES NO ONE.

THERE.

THERES NO ONE.

IVE GOT TO GET HIM.

THERES NO ONE FUCKING THERE.

My fuzzy eyes follow Uncle Alans back to the river and he is in and swimming front crawl and trying to stay in a straight line but the weir is pushing him left and Terry is crushing Leahs bones screaming ALAN! ALAN! ALAAAAN!!!

I try and see where Uncle Alan is swimming and there is no one in the water except when I close my eyes and that is when I see the back of a mans head.

It is Dads head I think and he is splashing like in the swimming pool in Rhodes and Uncle Alan keeps on getting closer but Dad or Dads Ghost or the man who looks like Dad keeps getting more far away and when I open my eyes again there is only Alan swimming to nowhere.

ALAAAAN!!!!

I try and move my head but it is still too heavy.

I am all too heavy. I dont even feel like I have a body it is like I am the river bank and the mud and I have been the mud for 2000 million years and I can see everything I can see Terry and

Leah on the river bank and Terry who is St Johns Ambulance pinching her nose and blowing in her mouth and he stops blowing and listens to her mouth and looks at Alan sinking under.

ALAAAAAN!!!!!

Leah wakes up from the dead and does a cough.

Terry says Girl girl youre all right youre all right.

St John holds up her head and the river comes out of her mouth and down her chin and he places her head down on the mud and turns her on her side facing me her eyes still sleeping.

He stands up and he runs to the edge and he unzips his tracksuit top and throws it off and he dives in and follows the whiteness Uncle Alan made in the water.

I try and lift my head. I try and get up. I am too tired. I am dead tired.

I see Leah with mud on one side of her face still looking dead and I think I am dead too.

We are the dead who arent buried properly on the banks of the river and we will stay here because the ferryman wont take us to the Underworld.

And then I see them.

They are standing there like the Furies. It is Ray Goodwin and the Victorian and Mr Fairview and all the Dead Fathers. They are all looking at me apart from Mr Fairview who is looking at Leah. And then Ray Goodwin in his check shirt and glasses looks at me with the Terrors in his face and he says The dead never rest Philip and his voice makes me sink into the mud and into sleep.

The People Who Come
and Sit on the Chair

The first is Mum who is holding her lips hard together like the whole world is trying to get out of her mouth.

I try and speak to her and tell her I am all right really and that I am just out of my body for a bit but she cannot hear me.

And then there is Leah in a dressing gown and hospital clothes and she calls me Stupid in a croak voice for jumping in after her and I am glad that she doesnt know the truth and then there is Mrs Fell who stays for ages and then there is Emperor Nero and his bleeding neck and he is playing his lyre and singing weird songs and then the chair is empty.

There is no one there and the hospital is dark and the Night Nurse walks by and the sound of her shoes on the floor goes all over the universe and I feel not in my body I am in everything and everyone is in everything they just dont know they are but they are because there are different levels of life.

There is the top level that is the level you see all the time and that is the level of all the lies and all the talking.

There is the second level that is the level of quietness and looks with eyes that are true and the tears that squeeze out of hugs and that is the level of love.

There is the third level that is the bits of your brain that scare you when shadows climb up the wall and when you stare at your face in the mirror until it isnt your face and that is the level of nightmares.

There is the fourth level that is the bits of you that you only see when you have to see them like when you are standing on a bridge and choosing to jump and that is the level of animals.

And then there is the bottom level that is the closest level to being dead and these are the parts of you that are not inside your body or your brain. These are the bits of you that are in everything. Like in the clouds and in the mud and you can move through all the world and all the universe when your body is still on a bed in a hospital and this is the level that doesnt have a name because words dont go that far down. They try but they cant reach but when you get higher you can hear the words falling down like a rope and you try and grab them and climb up through the levels.

Philip?
Philip?
Philip?
Philip?
Philip?
Philip can you hear me?
Philip?
Philip?
Philip?
Philip sweetheart can you hear me?
Philip?
Philip?
Philip?
Philip darling?
Philip?
Philip?
Its me darling.
Philip?
Philip?

The First Time I Wake Up

Sleep clings on my eyes like wet clothes trying to sink me down into the darkness.

She is holding my hand and she says Philip.

She says Philip can you hear me?

She says Philip sweetheart can you hear me?

I shout a Yes but it comes out like a whisper.

She says Philip youre all right. Youre in hospital but youre all right.

She smiles and the smile lets tears out of her eyes and they run down her face like it is a race to her chin.

She says I love you and she squeezes my hand and strokes it.

I say Leah.

She says What sweetheart?

I say Is Leah OK?

She says Yes. Yes she is. She left the hospital two hours ago. Shes fine. She left with her brother. She said shes going to New Zealand.

I say Uncle Alan.

She says What?

I say Is he OK?

She nods and she says Try and go back to sleep darling. The doctors say youll need to sleep.

I say Is he?

She says Try and sleep.

Philip?
Philip say something.
Philip?
Philip are you there?
Philip?
Philip please.
Philip talk to me.
Philip?
Philip I know you can hear me.
Philip?
Philip?
Philip?

The Second Time I Woke Up

Two nurses walked by and I looked at them walking free and I thought it must be weird being a nurse feeling lucky all the time to walk free and be well and not in pain. But then you might get sad because you know where life ends up.

Mum rubbed my hand and said The doctors say you can go home tomorrow.

I looked at the empty chair next to her and I said Wheres Uncle Alan?

Mum said Hes still here. Hes in a different part of the hospital.

She sucked her lips into her mouth and closed her eyes and this made me worry and I said Is he dead?

She said No really quick like if the word Dead was left in the air it would make it happen.

She said The doctors say he is doing well. He just hasnt woken up yet thats all.

I said It was two days ago.

She said I know Philip. I know. But its going to be all right. Hes going to be all right.

I didnt think anything was ever going to be all right but I said I know. Hell be all right.

Then Mum went in her Morrisons carrier bag that had the little oranges in and she got out the Newark Advertiser and said Theyve found them.

I said What?

She said Look and she gave me the paper.

I looked at the front page and the big writing said **PUB GANG CAUGHT**. There were pictures of three men Id never seen before and I started to read the story and it said

PUB LANDLORDS throughout the Newark and Sher-wood area will be able to sleep much more soundly tonight as the three men responsible for criminal damage and robbery at various local pubs have finally been arrested. The men were caught by a police rapid-response unit while breaking into the Turk's Head pub in Balder-ton, and have confessed to similar break-ins at the Robin Hood in Collingham, and the Castle and Falcon in Newark.

I looked at the pictures again and it was not Uncle Alan and it was not Sleepy Eye Terry.

And then after Mum went and left the small oranges I thought about other things like the fish tank and Sleepy Eye Terry letting go of my neck and all the things Dads Ghost had said all flashing in my head and I thought What is right and what is wrong? I tried to think of all the things I knew definitely and there were only six things I knew definitely and they were

Dad died on the bridge near Kelham

Three men came and smashed the Pub
My fish melted
Mr Fairview died in the fire at the Garage
Uncle Alan saved my life
Me and Uncle Alan and Sleepy Eye Terry saved Leahs life
And I thought about the melting fish. I thought it might not have been Uncle Alan. It might have been an accident. Mum might have knocked it when she was dusting and I blamed him like Emperor Nero blamed the Christians and the Romans blamed Nero and I looked round at all the ill people in the beds.

I thought about Ross and Gary and the trainers and Uncle Alan might have bought them for another reason I didnt know.

Mrs Fell came and saw me when Mum was visiting Uncle Alan.

She tilted her head more sideways than ever and said So how are you FEELING now Philip?

I said Im all right. But when I swallow I can still taste the river in my mouth.

Mrs Fell said Ew.

There was a big bit of no talking and I heard a plane going over the hospital and in my head I saw Leah and Dane on the plane and it was going to New Zealand to their aunts house by the sea.

Mrs Fell said Your uncles a very brave man isnt he Philip?

I smiled a Yes but couldnt say one.

She said Hes quite a hero. Just like his nephew.

I said I dont know.

She looked at me for a Long Time and read my face like it was a sad story.

I thought I could ask her anything now and she would tell me so I said Do you still think about your dad?

Her face went like cold water had landed on it and she said Of course I do Philip. I think about him every single day.

She laughed air out of her nose but in a sad way and she said Every time I go through the school gates.

I said Why?

She took a big breath and made her boobs go big and she said He always wanted me to be a Teacher Philip. I wanted to be an actress but he didnt like that idea very much.

I said Did you try and do acting?

She said I went to Drama School. But I left when I was 19.

I said Why?

She smiled but her face looked more sad and she said Thats when he died. I was in my First Year and I got a phone call from Mum telling me hed had a heart attack.

My head went all weird. I thought she was going to say Ray Goodwin was stabbed by a miner or shot by a gangster but shed said heart attack.

I said What?

She said He had a heart attack Philip. Hed had a lot of problems. And I felt bad. I felt guilty for making him worry about me. So I left Drama School and ended up learning how to be a Teacher. My mum said I should stay and do Drama but she was very ill herself so I went back home and looked after her and went to a Teachers Training College near Ollerton.

I didnt understand and I said But I thought he was

And I nearly said it I nearly said MURDERED but I didnt because I knew it would make her hate me and I knew a heart attack wasnt murder so I didnt need to ask.

Mrs Fell said The thing is Philip. There comes a time when you have to put the dead to rest Philip. When you have to trust the living instead. You cant live for your dad for ever Philip. When Dad died I believed it was all my fault. But I dont think that any more. You can believe what you want to believe. Thats what I think.

I said Like when Nero believed the Christians started the fire.

She said Yes. Like that.

I looked at Mrs Fell and she nodded her head like she was answering a question and then she said I showed the class a picture of him. Can you remember?

I said No.

She tucked a bit of her curly hair behind her ear and said When we did that lesson about Family Trees.

And that is when I worked out how I first knew about Ray Goodwin. It wasnt from Dads Ghost it was in the lesson on Family Trees the day before Dad died when Mrs Fell told us her Dad was a miner.

I could believe what I wanted to believe now so I wasnt going to believe in the Dead Fathers Club and I wasnt going to believe in ghosts that are in pain for ever if you dont help them.

Mrs Fell said But I suppose it worked out for the best. If I hadnt gone to be a Teacher I wouldnt have met Jonathan.

She lifted up her rings on her Wedding finger and I thought of the man she was with in the wheelchair who was ill.

Mrs Fell said with sadness in her eyes and happiness in her smile That reminds me. Id better be off.

She patted my hand and stood up to go and she said Trust the living Philip. Trust the living. Thats what I reckon.

And I said Yes.

Philip?
Philip?
Philip why cant you hear me?
Why cant you see me?
Im here Philip.
Im here right in front of you.
Philip look.
Please Philip.
Philip?
Philip?
Philip?
Im trapped Philip.
Im trapped inside this place.
Youve got to help me.
Youve got to let me out.

The Bird Out of the Window

Mum poured the black water out and made a puddle on the grass.

The water had bubbles in it that popped and the puddle got smaller and smaller because the grass was drinking it.

She put the clinky metal cup next to the grave again and poured new water out of the Pepsi bottle and then she put the metal lid with the holes in the cup. She cut the ends of the flowers and she started to put them through and she gave me some to do as well and I put the green stems inside the holes and the flowers bent their heads in their hoods. I tried to get them to point up to the sky but they kept on flopping their heads like they were at a flower funeral.

She said Leave them Philip. Theyre OK.

I said But they look better pointing up.

She said Theyre meant to be like that.

I said Oh.

She stood in front of the grave and said to it Happy Birthday.

And I said it too Happy Birthday.

Mum looked at Dad tucked up in the grass like he was sleeping under a duvet and I stood next to her and she rubbed my back.

It was nearly dark and we just looked at Dads grave a bit more and let the wind play our coats and play the trees.

Mum said Wed better go now Philip.

I said Yes.

She said Its nearly time to see Alan.

I said OK and then I said Bye to Dad.

And we went back on the path and there were two men digging a hole for a coffin and we got back to the car and Mum put the heater on and we drove out and left Dad under the grass and I looked at Mums face. It was worried about Uncle Alan and it was changing colour under the Christmas lights of Father Christmas and Snowmen and Rudolph and the North Star and the Angels and we passed the big Christmas tree near the castle wall and it had little white lights on it.

We got to the hospital and Mum parked and switched off the engine. She did a big breath and opened the door and we got out and started walking.

I said Mum did you lock the car?

She went back to the car and locked it and she said I dont know if Im coming or going I honestly dont.

We went in the hospital and passed an old woman who was yellow like a Simpson being pulled on a wheelie bed. I followed Mum down all the white corridors left and right and left and we went in a lift. A little girl was crying into her dads tummy and the dad was stroking the back of her head and there was a man in green and he was scratching his face like his fingers were matches that wouldnt go on fire.

The green man said What floor you after?

Mum said Three.

The green man pressed three and we went up in the lift with the little girl crying and ding the doors opened. We went out and there was a woman behind a desk and Mum said Hello.

The woman knew who she was because she said If youd like to take a seat Mrs Noble and Ill just check with the nurse if its all right to go through.

We sat on plastic chairs and waited under the tick tock clock and smelt the smells of the hospital. Plastic smells and clean smells and school floor smells and the smells of the family waiting on the other chairs. The family wasnt talking and my mum wasnt talking and I wasnt talking and the nurses writing on clipboards werent talking and the doctors coming out of the swing doors werent talking. It was like the quiet bodies on the beds in the little rooms all around had a not talking illness that was catching.

I looked at the bit of tinsel behind the womans desk and it was gold and a bit of it was falling down and there was another shiny gold thing saying HAPPY CHRISTMAS but the MAS was hanging down so it said HAPPY CHRIST.

I was thinking Mrs Fell was right. There are choices. You can listen to ghosts or you can not listen to ghosts and you can think what you want to think it is up to you because there are only two things that are true 100 out of 100 times and that is that you live and also that you die and every other thing is not true or false it is a mix. It is both. It is none.

And Mum was talking now.

She was saying I wonder why theyre taking so long. Normally I just go straight in.

There was a window and a small shape out of the window

and the small shape was a bird that was doing nothing just staying still.

A nurse came and said Are you waiting to go into Bay six?

Mum said Yes.

The nurse said You can both go through now. If youd like to follow me.

We followed her down the corridor and the nurse said Hello to a woman in a suit who walked past.

And then I saw him in the glass that was a rectangle in the wall. The glass made it look like he was in a fish tank and he was lying on a bed with a green blanket tucked round his big tummy and the nurse lifted her arm to the door and Mum went in the door and I went in the door.

He looked just normal like he was asleep but there were machines by him and wires coming out of him like he was a machine and he had a white clip on his finger and there was a screen making electric steeples with the heart beats beep beep beep.

Mum looked at him and she had wobbly breathing and she sat down on a chair next to the bed and I sat down on a chair next to it and I looked under the mask at Uncle Alans mouth open like he was waiting for someone to put a coin on his tongue to pay the man on the ferry to take him across the River Styx.

Mum talked to him like he could hear her.

She said I think you were right about the Christmas tree. It will look nice in the corner next to the machines. We can go to that place in North Muskham and choose one. Philips going to help arent you Philip?

I said Yes.

Mum said Carla and Nooks have helped put all the other decorations up. It looks really lovely doesnt it Philip?

I said Yes.

Mum was leaning forward with one hand on her chin and one hand over her knee like she was a number 4.

Uncle Alan did nothing. He just kept his eyes shut and his mouth open with no coin and the screen kept beeping beep beep beep.

There was a knock on the door and the door opened and a man in a long white coat and a long white face was there. I could tell Mum knew who he was and he said Mrs Noble if youve got five minutes Id like to just speak to you for a minute.

Mum went out and I stayed there. She didnt quite shut the door and some of the doctors words were thin and squeezed inside

serious

water

lungs

high

pox

ear

brain

swell

risk

damage

heart

Survive

60

per cent

choice

decision

breathing

breathing

breathing

Mrs Noble

The doctor kept on talking and Mum kept on not talking and I moved into Mums chair and it was warm from her bum. I looked at Uncle Alan and I looked at his big hand by his side and the wire going into his wrist. I touched his hand with my fingertips and it was real and it was warm and I didnt know if it was the hand that messed with Dads car but it was the hand that saved Leah and saved me and might have saved Mum and there were no marks on the hand. No oil from engines. It was all washed off in the river.

The doctor closed the door and stopped the words squeezing through.

I said Uncle Alan.

Uncle Alan said beep beep beep beep.

I said Im sorry about the PlayStation.

Uncle Alan said beep beep beep beep.

I said And everything.

Uncle Alan said beep beep beep beep.

I held his hand and watched the tube going into his mouth and the tube going into his blood.

I said You cant die Uncle Alan. Youve got to live. If you live Ill make it up to you. It will be great and we can be like a family and everything and we can have a nice Christmas.

Dads Ghost said inside my head Two minutes Philip. Two minutes to stop the Terrors.

I said Go away.

Dads Ghost said You are a fool Philip. You are a fool.

I said Go away.

Dads Ghost said I must rest. I cant stay in pain for ever.

I said Go away!

And I saw Uncle Alans eyes flicker and move like dinosaurs eggs when the baby dinosaurs are about to come out and I thought he was going to wake up but he didnt. His hand went twitchy so I put it down and then Dads Ghost came out of my brain and went inside the machine and down through wires in an air bubble like he was a Changemaker and the screen went beep beep beep beep beep beeeeeeeeeeeeeeeeeeeeeeeeeeeeeeeeeeeeeeeeeeee and the steeples went flat and I said Mum!

And Mum and the long white doctor came in and the doctor looked at the screen and then shouted out the open door in fast hospital language for people to come in.

And Mum was saying Whats happening? Whats happening? Whats going on?

The doctor went to the machines and then other people came in and the doctor said Mrs Noble wait outside both of you wait outside.

beeeeeeeeeeeeeeeeeeeeeeeeeeeeeeeeeeeeeeeeeeeeeeeeeeeeeeee

Me and Mum went outside the room and Mum was walking backwards and forwards and backwards and forwards and we could see him in the fish tank glass when they put the metal things on him trying to start him like an engine and Mum said Oh God oh please God oh God oh please please oh God and God said nothing.

I said Mum.

Mum said Oh God oh please.

I said Mum.

Mum said Oh Oh Oh.

I said Mum lets sit down come on Mum.

I held her hand that was cold and we walked to the chairs. There was no one there now except the bird out of the window and we sat down and Mums pink nails were digging into my skin. I did a prayer in my head and then after the prayer I wished I was a Roman because they had more Gods and they could keep saying prayers until there was a God who could help.

The bird turns its head in a jerk like a dinosaur and I think it looks at me with its eyes that dont blink and it flies off and into the sky which is too dark to see and the nails keep digging and I do nothing I just keep breathing in and out and in and out.